USA Today bestselling author Janice Maynard's sweet and sexy series continues, filled with love and adventure amid the ruggedly romantic setting of Scotland...

Bella is housesitting in Portree, Scotland, for her brother, Finley, while he's on his honeymoon. She expects a quiet time, enjoying the harbour town's breathtaking views and quaint shops. So imagine her surprise when one of Great Britain's most eligible bachelors comes pounding at her door in an attempt to evade both the paparazzi and a flurry of female fans. Unaware of his celebrity status, Bella reluctantly gives him sanctuary. Yet the surprises keep coming, and soon she's persuaded to accompany him to Edinburgh . . . as his faux fiancée. But while helping him fend off his ardent admirers, Bella just may gain one very authentic admirer of her own . . .

The Kilted Heroes series by Janice Maynard

Hot for the Scot

Scot of My Dreams

Not Quite a Scot

Scot on the Run

Also by Janice Maynard

By Firelight

Published by Kensington Publishing Corporation

Scot on the Run

The Kilted Heroes

Janice Maynard

LYRICAL SHINE
Kensington Publishing Corp.
www.kensingtonbooks.com

LYRICAL SHINE BOOKS are published by

Kensington Publishing Corp.
119 West 40th Street
New York, NY 10018

All Kensington titles, imprints, and distributed lines are available at special quantity discounts for bulk purchases for sales promotion, premiums, fund-raising, educational, or institutional use.

Special book excerpts or customized printings can also be created to fit specific needs. For details, write or phone the office of the Kensington Sales Manager: Kensington Publishing Corp., 119 West 40th Street, New York, NY 10018. Attn. Sales Department. Phone: 1-800-221-2647.

First Electronic Edition: July 2017
eISBN-13: 978-1-5161-0098-9
eISBN-10: 1-5161-0098-0

First Print Edition: July 2017
ISBN-13: 978-1-5161-0099-6
ISBN-10: 1-5161-0099-0

Printed in the United States of America

A special thank you to Martin Biro for bringing the Kilted Heroes series to life. I enjoy working with you!

Chapter One

"Seriously, Finley. I'll be fine. Quit worrying about me." Bella gazed at her sibling in amusement. He was so head over heels in love with his new bride and eager to get away on his honeymoon that his customary big brother routine was worse than usual. "I know how to take care of the dog," Bella said. "I'll deal with the bills and your business mail. I've got this. You and McKenzie don't need to worry about a thing."

McKenzie looked up from the suitcase she was packing. The gold, designer bikini in her hand was tiny. "Quit pestering your sister, Finley. Bella is a capable, grown woman." The slender blonde whose sophisticated image sometimes made Bella feel frumpy, dangled the bits of cloth in front of her husband's face. "Are three swimsuits enough, do you think, honey?"

Finley's eyes glazed over. He caught the brown-eyed blonde up in a ferocious hug. "You won't need *any* of them as far as I'm concerned."

Bella chuckled and slipped out of the room to give the newlyweds some privacy. The wedding ten days ago in Atlanta had been the social event of the season. The enormous Episcopal cathedral had barely managed to seat the crowd of two thousand.

Even though Bella and Finley's father owned a nationally recognized furniture manufacturing company, and even though they had grown up in North Carolina with every financial advantage, McKenzie's family's fortunes were on a whole different level. Bella had worn a bridesmaid dress by Vera Wang. The bride's wedding gown was Versace. A world-renowned stringed quartet played during the reception at an elite Buckhead country club. Champagne had flowed like water.

It was the most amazing wedding Bella had ever seen, certainly the fanciest one of which she'd ever been a part. Aside from all the hoopla, though, what Bella had enjoyed most was seeing her brother so happy. When Finley was with McKenzie, he was at peace with himself and his world.

More than a decade ago, Finley had left North Carolina after a bitter fight with their father. Finley had settled here on the Isle of Skye in Scotland and made a life for himself designing and selling custom-built motorcycles that were in demand all over the world. The rich and famous came to Skye in search of Bella's brother.

And now he had McKenzie. Bella's new sister-in-law was delightful. She was funny and smart and driven. McKenzie was the perfect match for Bella's taciturn brother.

Finley and McKenzie were heading to Greece for a month, leaving Bella in charge of the house and any little details that might crop up business-wise. She would be able to explore the countryside, putter around the town of Portree, and enjoy her newfound freedom now that the end of her many years of education was in sight.

She had missed Finley desperately while she had been in North Carolina and he had been in Scotland. They had lost their mother when they were young, their father far more recently. Bella looked forward to spending more time in Scotland in the future visiting her brother and sister-in-law. Plus, Finley and McKenzie were making plans to spend half of every year in Atlanta, so Bella would be able to see them often, even if she was still living in North Carolina.

Finally, three hours later, the suitcases were all packed and the last minute instructions disseminated. Bella stood at the door and waved as Finley's car disappeared down the hill. McKenzie stuck an arm out the window and waved back madly.

After that, Bella was alone.

The momentary letdown she felt was understandable. It had been a heck of a month. But now she had oodles of time ahead of her to tick off every single thing on her to-do list. Scotland awaited.

"Come on, girl," she said to the dog. "Let me get your leash, and we'll go for a walk."

* * *

During the next two weeks, Bella's days fell into a pattern. After breakfast each morning she spent some time journaling. She had a couple of big decisions to make in the coming months. Staring at a blank page forced her to deal with her doubts and misgivings, as well as her goals and dreams.

The afternoons were usually her time to explore the countryside. For now, she limited her excursions to the Isle of Skye. There would be plenty of time to go farther afield. In the meantime, she fell in love with this moody gem of the Scottish Highlands.

Cinnamon turned out to be the perfect housemate. The dog slept on the floor beside the bed each night. Although Bella was perfectly content to be on her own, she came to rely on the canine's comforting presence and was happy to have the company.

Even if there was a certain amount of monotony in her quiet, introspective days, Bella wouldn't have put that in the negative column. Being able to do what she wanted *when* she wanted was amazingly freeing after years of slavishly following an academic calendar.

She had begun to think nothing out of the ordinary was ever going to come along to disturb her peaceful existence, but all that changed one warm, late-summer morning. She had come downstairs to return a borrowed book to the shelf when a raucous pounding sounded at the front door.

More startled that anything else, she peeked out the tiny window set high up in the door. The unexpected visitor saw her and began to yell and gesticulate.

"Let me in, lass! They're right behind me."

Chapter Two

Bella kept the chain fastened and peeked through the opening at the large, agitated man on her doorstep. She knew the town of Portree was about as safe as any place on the planet. Still, she wasn't inclined to be naïve when a stranger showed up demanding entrance.

"Hurry," the man said, looking frantically over his shoulder. "I know your brother. I bought a motorcycle from him. Finley knows I'm here. I'm harmless, I swear. For God's sake, let me in!"

Maybe it was the urgency in the man's voice or the wonderful Scottish cadence of his speech. Perhaps it was hearing her brother's name. Whatever the reason, Bella slipped the chain free of its mooring and opened the door. The tall lanky man brushed past her, his gaze darting around the room.

"You'd better hide out in the kitchen," she said calmly. "Who exactly is after you?"

"Reporters." He shuddered, his expression hunted.

"Right…" She drawled the word, wondering if her unexpected guest suffered from mental health issues. He made a definite impression, not only for his height and odd circumstances, but because he was gorgeous. There was no other way to describe it. His thick chestnut hair had a little cowlick at the crown. It was shaggy as if he needed a haircut.

Eyes the color of moss were framed in thick dark lashes. Broad shoulders strained the seams of a forest-green Henley shirt. He looked like the kind of man who could climb a mountain or tunnel out of a prisoner-of-war camp in an old movie. In other words, not her type at all.

Cataloging her guest's features had to be put on hold when a ferocious knocking at the door made her wince.

The mystery man grabbed both of her hands in his, the grip firm and warm. "I beg you, Finley's sister. For the love of God, give me asylum." Staring into those eyes made her pulse flutter. Refusing to be won over by something so superficial as masculine charm, she cocked her head toward the kitchen doorway. "Stay in there. Don't make a sound."

When he disappeared, she wiped her palms on the legs of her jeans and took a deep breath. This time she opened the door all the way as if she had nothing to hide. "May I help you?" she asked pleasantly.

Two short, stocky men carrying fancy cameras stared past her intently. The professional-grade lenses of their cameras were huge. They could probably see footsteps on the moon. Or photograph film stars frolicking nude on a hidden beach. Bella had been a child when Princess Diana died fleeing paparazzi. She didn't know what her mystery guest had done to deserve this treatment, but in an instant, she was on his side.

Bella repeated her question. "May I help you?"

"We're looking for a bloke. Six three, brown hair, green eyes."

She smiled gently. "Sounds hard to miss. But sorry. I can't help you." She settled herself in the doorway more deliberately as the men became restive.

One of them frowned. "Are you saying you haven't seen him? He was running up this hill, and yours is the only house up here."

"I would think if he were being chased..." She lifted her nose and grimaced. "He could have doubled back and headed down to the harbor. We've all sorts of boats down there, you know. I imagine your quarry is out on the water and long gone by now."

For the first time, the reporters looked crestfallen, but no more so than the gaggle of women standing behind them. "You swear you haven't seen him?"

Under oath, or confronted with a uniformed officer, she might have replied differently. Given the circumstances, she chose to sin by omission. "Good day, gentlemen. And good luck with your hunt."

Then she closed the door in their faces. Leaning her back against it, she ran a trembling hand over her damp forehead. "You can come out now," she said.

Her fugitive returned from the kitchen, his body language a mix of sheepish relief and guilt. "Thank you, Finley's sister. You've saved me. I'm Ian Larrimore."

She pointed at an armchair by the fireplace. "Sit there and don't move a muscle until I've talked to my brother."

"Yes, ma'am." His hangdog expression was patently false. Nevertheless, he did as she asked.

Finley answered on the third ring, his voice slightly grumpy. Bella didn't care. Finley had a bad habit of playing matchmaker where his little sister was concerned. If this was one of his elaborate schemes to put eligible men in her path, she would nip that in the bud immediately.

Ian picked up a magazine and flipped through it, seemingly unconcerned. Bella stepped into the kitchen and lowered her voice, keeping an eye on the intruder. "What's going on, Finley? There's a man here who claims he knows you. Ian Larrimore? Does that ring a bell?"

"Of course it does."

"Tell me the truth. Is this a set-up? Did you think I was going to be lonely here without you?"

"Ian's in trouble," Finley said, clearly avoiding the question. "I told him he could lay low for a few weeks in the guest room."

On the surface, the explanation seemed feasible. Finley's home was listed on the island's B&B registry. At Finley's suggestion, Bella was sleeping in the master suite while bride and groom were traveling, so the guest room was available. Still, Bella was suspicious.

She lowered her voce even further. "What's wrong with him? Why is he in trouble? I don't want to get mixed up in something illegal."

Finley sighed, his disgust coming through loud and clear even across the miles. "Give me some credit, Sis. It's nothing like that. Do you have your laptop handy?"

She frowned. "Yes. It's here on the kitchen table. Why?"

"Google Ian's name. It's easier than me trying to explain."

With Ian seemingly engrossed in a motorcycle magazine, Bella sat down and switched the phone to her left hand. With her free hand, she typed in what she needed and stared at the top hit. It was the website for a well-known entertainment magazine. Not one of the nastier tabloids, but simply a pop culture, lots-of-photographs publication.

The lead story was hard to miss. *Meet the twenty most eligible bachelors in Great Britain.* She sighed audibly. "Seriously, Finley? You stuck me with a society playboy?" Ian's name was number two. Prince Harry, understandably, had snagged the top slot. Hard to compete with royalty.

"It's not like that, Bella. Ian's a scientist. An engineer. He hates all the attention. It's ruined his life. All I'm asking is that you let him hide out for a couple of weeks 'til this blows over."

"Your trip to Greece was supposed to also be *my* six weeks of peace and quiet. So I could work on my research. You're not playing fair, Finley."

She loved nothing more than solitude and getting lost in her books.

"He won't get in your way, I swear. The man's as much of a hermit-nerd as you are."

"Hermit-nerd? That's a bit insulting, don't you think?"

"Are you saying it isn't true?"

Her brother's teasing made her smile reluctantly. "No. But I'm still miffed at you. If I find out you're trying to marry me off again, you're in big trouble."

"Never crossed my mind," Finley swore. "You and Ian are too much alike. It would never work. His IQ might even be higher than yours. I shudder to think what your offspring would be like. They'd probably come out of the womb talking in complete sentences."

"Can we please quit discussing my reproductive organs and get back to the fact that you double-booked your house?"

"What was I going to do, Bella? The man was desperate."

"Fine." She sighed, closing her computer. "But you owe me for this one."

"No problem. My lovely wife has already picked out some ridiculously expensive Greek jewelry to bring back to you."

"It may take more than shiny baubles to make up for this."

"Whatever you say. Relax, Bella. Ian is harmless. You won't even know he's there."

Bella ended the call and stood in the doorway, assessing her new guest. At the moment, he seemed perfectly calm and content. Not at all like the man she had met half an hour ago.

She joined him in the other room, wishing she had put on something more impressive than faded jeans and an old college T-shirt that morning. "Finley vouched for you. And he explained about the whole magazine thing. I suppose I have no choice but to allow you to stay. It's not my house, after all."

"I'm sorry to put you out," Ian said with a lopsided smile that conveyed remorse and regret. "I'll try to stay out of your way."

Since the man was well over six feet tall and exuded raw, shiver-inducing sex appeal, Bella found that highly unlikely. "A few ground rules," she said tartly. "No loud music."

"I use headphones."

"You clean up after yourself in the kitchen."

"I'm a neat freak."

"No more asking me to lie to the paparazzi."

Ian stood and stretched. The bottom edge of his shirt rode up, revealing two inches of flat, hard, tanned masculine abdomen. "I understand, lass.

'Twas not fair of me. But in my defense, that ravening pack of wolves has been at my heels for the past two weeks. I haven't been able to leave my flat. My mail has been filled with strange boxes…women sending me their underwear…" He trailed off, shuddering and wincing.

"I assume you have to be rich to make that list," Bella said. "Don't tell me you have a title, too."

He shook his head. "No, thank the Lord. I come from a very ordinary small village outside of Glasgow. The only reason I made that bloody bachelor list is because I patented a rescue apparatus that was picked up by the Royal Navy and others. Turned out to be lucrative. That wasn't why I did it. The money's still in the bank. I'm jabbering. I'll shut up now. In my defense, I'm not very good at small talk."

Bella stared at him, feeling her heart do a funny flip. Clearly money wasn't the only reason Ian Larrimore had landed on the eligible bachelor list. Either he was being modest, or he truly was as endearingly humble as he seemed. Surely a man as smart as he was could take an honest look in the mirror.

"Where do you live now?" she asked.

"London. And you?"

"North Carolina. In the States."

"I hear it's lovely there."

"It is."

Good grief. Nothing like two introverts to get a conversation buzzing. This was exactly why she liked being alone. People were so much work, especially people of the opposite sex. She ran her hands through her hair. "Where is your luggage?"

His cheeks reddened. "I abandoned my car on a side street in town. I'll sneak out after dark and retrieve it."

"Okay."

Ian shifted from one foot to the other. He was so tall he dwarfed the low-ceilinged space. Finley had inherited this quaint and cozy house from its previous owner, an old man who needed help with chores. He had given Finley room and board years ago in exchange for an able-bodied young man's help with things that were too difficult for him to manage.

Ian picked up his high-end leather backpack. "I'm assuming Finley has Wi-Fi. If you'll point me to my quarters, I'll get out of your hair."

The man's Scottish accent was a delight. Now that Bella was surrounded by the speech patterns of the Highlands on a daily basis, you'd think she would have become immune to the wonderful cadences of the native tongue. But it wasn't so. Hearing Ian's mundane words was like listening to poetry.

Bella nodded. "Of course. Follow me." As she led him up the narrow stairs, she was ruefully aware that her days of wandering around the house each morning in a T-shirt and undies were over. If she wanted to get up and read at three in the morning, she'd have to be careful not to let the stairs creak when she tiptoed down to the kitchen for a cup of tea.

Darn Finley and his careless hospitality! Already, Bella had begun to feel a sense of ownership in this delightful house. With her brother gone for an entire month, she had plenty of time to play tourist and write and dream.

Now it wouldn't be the same at all.

She stepped aside to let Finley enter the immaculate guest room. Although not luxurious, the space was comfy and appealing. "You're lucky Cinnamon wasn't here," Bella said suddenly. "She's at the dog groomer, but she wouldn't have been too happy about me letting a stranger through the front door."

"Cinnamon?"

"She's a beautiful English Cocker."

"Ah, yes. I met her last year…when I came to pick up my bike."

Bella's brother built one-of-a-kind, incredibly expensive motorcycles. His usual clients were movie stars and royalty. Ian must be extremely comfortable financially to be able to afford such a toy. That fact didn't impress her in the least. She'd had plenty of opportunities to discover a man's bank balance wasn't a good indicator of his character.

She held out her hand. "I think you'll find everything you need. I'll dig out a spare house key for you later on and leave it on the hall table."

Her guest nodded, making her feel unaccountably guilty. His green eyes crinkled at the corners. "Thank you." He paused and grimaced. "I assume your last name is Craig? But I don't know your first name."

"It's Bella. Short for Arabella. That was too much of a mouthful, so my parents shortened it."

He tested the mattress with one hand. "Bella. The name suits you."

There was no overt flattery in his tone or expression, but the words were definitely a compliment. Which left Bella flustered and out of sorts. "I have work to do," she said. "Make yourself at home."

She fled to her room, remembering for no particular reason the miserable day before her senior prom when Dusty Bennett decided at the last minute to take a date who was blonder and dumber than Bella. He'd told her guys didn't like girls who were too smart.

Even then Bella had recognized what a total ass he was. But the careless rejection hurt nevertheless. She'd spent half a decade trying to *be* smart without letting anyone know. In the end, the playacting had become too much of a burden. She was who she was.

Even so, really handsome men made her nervous. She preferred nerds, as her brother so blithely described them. Male or female, they were *her* people. It wasn't that she thought superficial social interactions and pop culture were unimportant. It was just that she had so many other things that interested her.

In the bathroom she splashed water on her hot cheeks and brushed her hair. Staring into the mirror she faced a woman who was average for the most part. Her eyes were large and a nice shade of blue. A nose that was a bit off center. A chin that was more sharp than feminine.

She did like her hair…most days. It was thick and healthy and required little effort on her part to be presentable. Although she had been known to use a curling iron and hairspray on special occasions, most days she simply caught it up in a ponytail and went about her business.

Suddenly, as she sifted through memories of the past half hour, something about Ian's appearance surprised her. Though he was striking enough to be a film star, his clothes struck an odd note. The tweed jacket he wore was frayed at the cuffs and an inch too short for his long arms. His pants were wrinkled. Even his socks were mismatched.

It had been a very long time since a man had interested Bella in any way other than cerebrally. Ian Larrimore might have an impressive brain, but it wasn't his IQ that was getting her all hot and bothered.

This was a very inconvenient time for her hormones to go haywire. She was here to work on her dissertation. To soak up the history hidden in the rocks and the hills, to immerse herself in the magic that was Scotland.

She definitely didn't need a man to distract her from her goals.

Fortunately, Ian seemed set on making her dislike him from the start. When she went downstairs at six that evening to make herself a sandwich and a cup of tea, he showed up in the kitchen with an envelope in his hand. "This is for you," he said, prowling around the small room with the old-fashioned appliances.

The envelope was full of twenty pound notes. She frowned. "I don't understand."

The man with the supposedly stratospheric IQ shrugged. "I don't know how to cook. In London I order take away. That's not really much of an option here in Portree. I can't expect you to absorb the cost of feeding me. So I'm compensating you for your trouble and expense."

Bella's ire began to simmer. "You want me to feed you?"

Ian's green-eyed gaze was guileless. "Well, if you're going to prepare meals for yourself, I assumed it wouldn't be that much of a bother to double the recipes. I'd be ever so grateful."

Bella pushed her chair back from the table and stood, wishing she were half a foot taller so she could spit in his eye. "Unbelievable," she said. "I'm a woman, therefore I must be willing and able to cook. Is that what you're implying?"

"I meant no disrespect. The ability to cook is a valuable skill."

"But a feminine one." He should have been alarmed by the ice in her voice, but the poor man forged ahead anyway.

"Aye. It's often the lasses who are best at it. I wouldn't know. My own mum ran away when I was a young child. My father hired a combination nanny/housekeeper to look after us. She was no dab hand in the kitchen, I'll tell you, but at least we didn't go hungry."

The fact that Ian had lost his mother at a young age just as Bella had lost hers slowed her down for half a second, but she was too riled up to make peace now. She shoved the puffy envelope against his chest, forcing him to grab for it. "Well, I suppose you'll go hungry, Mr. Larrimore. I'm not your mother, your nanny, nor your housekeeper. So I'd suggest you learn how to fry an egg."

Chapter Three

Ian winced as the kitchen door slammed hard enough to rattle the glassware in the cabinets. What had he said to upset her?

Slumping into a chair at the table, he drummed his fingers on the scratched wooden surface. This was his punishment for trying to run away from the insane press attention in London. Now here he was, trapped in a small house in the back of beyond with a woman who thought he was an idiot.

He never had been very good at personal relationships. His father raised him mostly in absentia, and the old man definitely hadn't believed in coddling children. Ian had spent a lot of time on his own, particularly after he was old enough to dispense with the babysitter after school.

His stomach growled loudly, dragging him back to the present. He pondered his choices. There were a number of nice seafood restaurants in Portree. But after today's harrowing sprint, he wasn't yet ready to tangle with the paparazzi again. That meant invading lovely Bella's refrigerator without an invitation. He had already incurred her displeasure. Surely this would be a minor infraction.

Even after raiding the fridge, his choices were limited. Either Bella subsisted on yogurt and Swiss cheese, or she went out for many of her meals. Fortunately, she had apparently brought her own stash of peanut butter, which Ian had learned to love while in the States. In the end, he fixed himself two PB&J sandwiches with strawberry jam and washed them down with a large glass of milk.

When he was done, he decided to go for a run. It was almost dark. No one would bother him. Then he remembered that his gear was still in his car. Hell. Now he had no choice but to retrieve his things. He would need to go and come on foot. To move the car to Bella's driveway would be the equivalent of a huge neon sign announcing his presence.

Even accessing his car in the dark was taking a chance.

Fortunately, the cluster of reporters who had followed him from Inverness must have been convinced he had left by boat or else they were too tired to venture out at night. Ian was able to unlock the boot of his car and grab his two bags without incident.

He trudged back up the hill to Finley's house wondering why the man hadn't bothered to tell his lovely sister he had issued an invitation to the most hunted man in the UK at the moment. Ian snorted aloud, incredulous that his life had come to this. He should have stayed in London, perhaps, but he was tired of holing up in his flat. He missed the days when he could run and bike and walk in pleasant anonymity. One bloody magazine article and now his whole ordered existence was shot to hell.

The house was dark when he returned. He had left the front door unlocked, since he didn't yet have a key. His hostess's room was on the third level of the dwelling, so he had no way of knowing if she was still awake or not.

The structure was built into the side of a hill. At one time it might have been two separate houses. Now it jumbled together drunkenly, as if trying to climb the incline on its own.

He changed clothes and laced up his shoes. Despite the hour, adrenaline surged in his veins. He felt as if he could run a marathon.

The small town of Portree was built like an elongated bowl, sliding from higher ground all the way down to the harbor. Ian pushed himself hard, relishing the punishing elevation changes. Sweat dampened his shirt. His heart pounded in his chest. Every bit of accumulated frustration he'd endured in the days since the article was published gradually winnowed away.

In the dark crystal-clear night, he found a measure of peace.

When he was spent, he made the climb back up to Finley's house. It didn't take a genius to know that part of his earlier mood could be attributed to sexual frustration. He wasn't the kind of man who enjoyed one-night stands. They left him feeling empty inside, despite the physical release.

On the other hand, he rarely had the time or the inclination to invest in a relationship with the kind of woman who might stick around. That meant he usually immersed himself in his work until he was too exhausted to do more than fall into bed and go to sleep.

Staying in Finley's house presented a new problem. In many ways, it was perfect. He had managed to elude reporters for the moment.

Unlike London, the Isle of Skye was peaceful and charming, a low-key environment that lent itself to serious endeavors.

But what was he going to do about Bella?

His reluctant hostess was prickly and argumentative and sexy as hell. Already, she fascinated him. Was there a boyfriend in the picture?

After he showered and eventually climbed beneath the covers, he found himself fixated on the image of his housemate upstairs in her own bed. Was she nude? Did she sleep in frilly, feminine nighties? Her skin was fair, smooth as a magnolia blossom. The faint hint of a southern belle accent made him wonder what her husky voice would sound like in the throes of passion…calling out his name.

He shifted on the mattress and cursed. With one snippet of a fantasy, he had erased all the benefits of his run. He was hard now…everywhere. And he ached for a woman. One particular woman with the face of an angel and the personality of a cactus. Taking matters into his own hands, he found release and drifted at last into a restless sleep.

* * *

Bella awoke at dawn feeling guilty. The fact that she *felt* guilty made her mad. Every morning since her brother and McKenzie had left on their honeymoon, Bella had awakened in perfect harmony with the world in general and the little hamlet of Portree in particular.

She had sipped her tea and jotted notes and played with the adorable Cinnamon. Now everything was ruined.

An apology was in order, though there was a good chance it might stick in her throat. Finley had invited his friend to stay. Fair or not, that was the reality. In Finley's absence, Bella was the de facto host. She had been touchy and rude yesterday, and she needed to make amends.

By the time Ian appeared in the doorway of the kitchen, yawning and stretching, she had rehearsed her speech a dozen times. When she saw her houseguest, her stomach curled and she caught her breath. *Holy Queen of Scots.* He was all warm and rumpled and sleepy-eyed. She wanted to gobble him up or wrestle him to the ground and kiss him from head to toe.

The man was a walking, talking romance hero. That was saying a lot coming from a woman who didn't believe in romance. She cleared her throat and tried to ignore the way his faded jeans rode low on his narrow hips. Today's soft Henley shirt was baby blue.

"Good morning, Ian," she said pleasantly. "I've fixed sausage and eggs. There's plenty for two. May I serve you a plate?"

He blinked owlishly. "Umm…"

"Oh, sit down," she said impatiently. "I'm trying to apologize. I wasn't at my best yesterday. I'm sorry. Of course I'll feed you. But I don't need your money. The number two bachelor in Great Britain is safe from me."

"Did anyone ever tell you you're not a warm fuzzy woman?" He sat down at the table and put his head in his hands with a little groan.

"As a matter of fact, yes." She tapped his shoulder. "Tea?"

"Do you have coffee?" he asked, the words muffled. "I went to the States for one of my degrees, and I picked up the habit."

"No problem. Did you hit the pub last night?" she asked, wondering if he really had a hangover.

"No." He sat up and scrubbed his face with his hands. "I had a hard time sleeping. The bed was perfectly comfortable," he said quickly, "but I'm a creature of habit. I never rest as well on the road as I do at home."

"I know exactly what you mean," Bella said. "It took me a full week to get over jet lag and to feel at ease in Finley's room. Now I love it, though."

Ian was quiet as she poured his coffee and prepared his plate. She had made an early morning run to the market for supplies. If a woman needed to grovel, a hot breakfast seemed an auspicious way to start.

After pouring herself a cup of coffee, she joined him at the table. "Here's the thing," she said. "I have a chip on my shoulder about the whole women-as-homemakers thing."

He shot her a sideways glance and gulped down half of the coffee. The man must have asbestos lungs.

"Okay."

"Okay, what?" she asked.

"Okay, nothing. You made a statement. I let you know I heard it."

"Don't try to *handle* me, Larrimore."

He held up one finger, still drinking from his coffee cup as if he had found the elixir of eternal life. "I wouldn't dream of it. And for the record, I don't have a mother or sisters, so I plead *not guilty* to having preconceived notions about the female sex."

"What about babies?"

He choked on his drink and coughed until his face turned red. "Babies?"

"You know. Loud. Poopy. Impossible to predict. If you and your wife had a baby, would you expect her to drop everything and play *mama*, or would you take an equal role?"

Ian set down his cup with exaggerated care and gave her a narrow-eyed look that indicated she might have gone a wee bit too far. "I'd say it's a bit early in our relationship to be discussing something so personal, lass. For the record, we Scots are a hospitable people, but not *that* hospitable. All I need is a bed and breakfast. I'm not expecting you to bear my children."

Bella gaped. It was her turn to blush. "We were having an academic discussion," she muttered, unable to meet his eyes. "I was curious about your opinions."

It seemed she has misjudged Ian Larrimore rather badly. Apparently, he was neither passive nor sexually repressed. The light in his eyes at the moment made her toes curl.

"Let me be clear," he said. "Babies come from sex, so if a woman starts talking procreation, a man's brain goes straight to the bedroom. If ye aren't making any kind of serious offer, I suggest you change the subject."

Unfortunately, she had used up all of her best conversational material. Now all she could think about was seeing Ian Larrimore in her bed, naked, ready to make babies with her. "I should get to work," she said, standing so abruptly her chair wobbled. "Don't worry about the kitchen. I'll tidy up later."

* * *

Ian finished his breakfast and lingered to enjoy a second cup of coffee. Often, when he was in the midst of a project, he became so engrossed he forgot to stop for lunch. That made the first meal of the day all the more important.

This morning, though, his thoughts were focused on something far more titillating than any experiment or computer program. He was fixated on Bella Craig. The way she smelled, like lavender and fresh air. Her rapid fire conversation that kept him on his toes. The delightfully feminine curves of her breasts and bottom. Head to toe, she was an exceptional female.

Too bad she was only here for a visit.

After breakfast, Ian retreated to the guest room, set up all of his equipment, and configured it to connect with the wireless network. Finley had spared no expense in this area, a decision Ian endorsed wholeheartedly. Good communication frameworks were a must in the twenty-first century.

When he had everything up and running to his satisfaction, he checked his e-mail, answered a few pressing queries, and then read the London papers online. In every instance, there were stories about Ian and his life and work. The invasion of privacy gave him indigestion. Why did anyone care?

He opened a program on his laptop and tried to concentrate, but he was disgruntled and frustrated. It was his custom to spend hour upon hour in isolation. Some of his best ideas and breakthroughs came when he was in the zone, all alone. Which made it all the more peculiar to realize he was curious about his American hostess.

Questions. So many questions. He had heard Finley mention his sister on one occasion or another, but Ian had never paid too much attention. All he remembered was that she was supposed to be very smart and that she was obsessed with European History, Great Britain's in particular.

At last, he settled into his routine. But he'd only been at it an hour when he heard a crash in the kitchen accompanied by loud barking. After lurching to his feet, he stumbled down the stairs and came to a halt in the doorway. The urge to laugh was almost uncontrollable, but he squelched it.

"Need a hand?" he asked, his question utterly uninflected.

Bella stared up at him. She was kneeling on the floor cleaning up broken glass. Cinnamon had apparently jumped up on the table and sent crockery flying. "Do you even have to ask?" The unrepentant dog sat at her hip, tongue lolling happily. An expensive leather leash lay abandoned nearby.

Ian crouched to pet the beautiful animal. "What's all the commotion about, big fella?"

"She's a girl. So there's that. And apparently, she thinks I'm going to be a pushover and let her run around outside without a leash."

Cinnamon flirted shamelessly, not even making a pretense of protecting her mistress from the big, bad stranger. "Such a sweet baby," Ian crooned as he tickled the dog behind her ears.

"Oh, good grief..."

Ian extended a hand to help Bella to her feet and watched as she emptied the dustpan into the waste basket. Though her fingers were small and delicate in his much larger palm, nothing about her indicated a lack of strength. Quite the opposite.

He released her immediately, though it went against the grain. "I wondered if you might be up for a drive," he said.

Bella seemed shocked. "I thought you had work to do."

"I *always* have work to do," he said with a laugh that held little humor. "But it's a beautiful day and you're..." He stopped abruptly, wary of coming on too strong.

"I'm what?"

Still the suspicious frown.

He'd almost said *you're a beautiful woman.* Instead, he took a less volatile conversational path. "You're here to see Scotland. Shouldn't you be out and about?"

"A fair point," she conceded, as if in the midst of a Supreme Court battle, "but what about your paparazzi?"

"They're not mine," he protested.

"You know what I mean."

"I'll wear a hat. And sunglasses. We'll take back roads."

"*Everything* here is a back road," she said wryly.

"C'mon, woman. Say yes." He halted abruptly and felt his ears get hot.

Bella, always prickly, noticed immediately. "What's wrong?"

He shrugged. "I just realized I don't actually have a car up here. You'd have to drive."

"Is that a problem for you? A woman behind the wheel?"

Her indignant question made him roll his eyes. "I'm as much of a feminist as the next guy…or woman, for that matter. So how about not assuming the worst about me every time I open my mouth?"

His retort was sharper than he had intended.

Bella blinked. "You're right. I'm sorry. It's sort of a knee-jerk reaction because of my dad and a couple of other chauvinist specimens. Perhaps we could agree to a détente while we get to know each other."

"I'm not the one who's tossing around allegations of misogyny."

"Okay, okay. You've made your point. Shall we take food with us, or shall we be spontaneous?"

"I suggest a compromise. Apples and crackers for a snack with the option of stopping at the other end of the island for dinner if we're in the mood."

"Sounds like a plan. I'll meet you back here in ten." Her sunny smile caught him off guard and told him he had far underestimated her appeal.

As he gathered his wallet and the few other things he might need for the island's mercurial weather, he told himself not to get too invested. Bella was an American with a life back in the States. Ian, God willing, would soon be returning to London and a pleasantly humdrum existence.

Not to mention the fact that Finley was Ian's friend. He would skin Ian alive if Ian tried to make a move on Bella. Even if Bella reciprocated, it would be a stupid thing to do. Which didn't explain why the thought of spending a platonic day with her was so damn exciting.

Bella drove like she talked. Point A to Point B with no rabbit trails. She played tour guide for him, sharing the history and significance of local points of interest. Her descriptions were vivid and concise. She would make a wonderful university professor. He wondered if that was what she had in mind for her future.

He didn't have the heart to tell her he had actually visited Skye before, twice in fact. And to be honest, not much had changed in the interim.

At his suggestion, they climbed several rock formations and at last sat down to enjoy the view. The clouds were high today and the visibility was good. In the distance, sunlight glinted off white caps and turned the water a shade of blue that matched Bella's eyes.

Finley's decision to live here made sense. It was a place where a man could breathe…a land close to the roots of civilization, close to the bounty of the sea. Ian leaned back on his hands and studied his companion out of the corner of his eye. She had scaled the steep hillside without complaint, and scarcely breathed hard in doing so.

He had tried over the years to be sensitive to women's issues. Certainly he believed in equal pay for equal work. Yet, suddenly, he could see how a woman who looked like Bella might have trouble gaining acceptance into the sometimes stodgy environs of the academic community.

She had referred in passing to men who had treated her badly. Who were those faceless men? Boyfriends? Colleagues?

Ian wasn't naïve. He knew many men who wanted to go out with women who were soft and amenable and not inclined to steal a man's thunder. Ridiculous nonsense, but there it was.

Bella Craig was smart and funny and surprisingly self-aware. Had she been hurt by someone who diminished her self-worth by discounting her intelligence? He found himself righteously indignant on her behalf without knowing the slightest thing about her circumstances.

"So tell me," he said. "What is it you're working on while you're housesitting for your brother?"

Bella's profile never changed. She gazed out into the distance as if her thoughts were miles away. Finally, she shrugged. "I was hoping to start my dissertation, but I wasn't able to nail down a topic before I left home. History should be vibrant and alive. I don't want to be the person who reduces it to a few dry chapters bound and stuck away in a university library."

"And therein lies your problem, I suppose."

She wrinkled her nose. When she half turned to face him, her small smile was wry and tentative. "If I tell you something, will you promise not to laugh?" Her knees were raised to her chest, arms tucked around them.

"I swear, lass." He mimed locking his lips and throwing away the key. "I'll take your secrets to my grave."

Chapter Four

His sober promise made Bella smile. "It's nothing so dramatic."

"Then tell me."

She pursed her lips, still unsure of him. "Never mind."

"Ach, lovely Bella. Don't be a tease. You've got my imagination running amok."

"I love it that you know what that word means."

"Are you calling me a nerd?"

"I would if I didn't think you would take it as a compliment."

"Touché, lass. You know me well already."

They were flirting. She knew it, and she could see by the warm intimate look in his eyes that he knew it as well. It wasn't a skill she had ever really mastered, but with Ian she didn't feel the frozen awkwardness that hobbled her in other intimate situations.

Despite his looks and his inclusion on that much-maligned list of bachelors, Ian was easy to be with. Real. Honest.

It would crush her if that impression turned out to be false.

"Okay," she said. "I guess I have to say it now. My field of study has narrowed to the evolution of courtship and marriage rituals among the aristocracy from the seventeenth to eighteenth centuries."

"Is this the part where I try not to laugh? Sounds very reasonable to me. Not that I'm fully cognizant of acceptable doctoral topics in the history department."

"It's a fine topic. Suitably boring. I'm ninety percent sure it will be approved if I write up the proposal and submit it."

"Then what's the problem?"

She took a deep breath, her stomach flipping and flopping as her cheeks heated. Even Finley knew nothing about this pipedream. "I'm not excited about a dissertation. I want to write a novel instead."

A long silence ensued. Apparently, Ian liked to think before speaking. Another point in his favor, even if it left her dangling in limbo.

He sat up and brushed off his hands. "Interesting."

A hot blush worked its way from her throat to her hairline. She angled her head away from him, pretending to study a ship out in the horizon. Her eyes stung, though she didn't know why. She had shared something intensely personal with a virtual stranger. What had she expected?

"We should go now," she said abruptly. "It's getting late, and I'm hungry. I want to grab an early dinner and get back to the house."

Before she could shoot to her feet and head down the hill, Ian caught her wrist in a gentle grasp. "I hurt your feelings. Or made you angry. Or something. I'm sorry, Bella. Talk to me, please." His voice was low, his words urgent. "I'm a clumsy oaf when it comes to this kind of thing. I had a very short-lived relationship in college with a woman who told me I had the emotional dexterity of a block of wood. I'm afraid she was right. I understand algorithms and equations, but I'm tone deaf when it comes to deciphering the nuances and subtext of conversation. Especially with women."

Bella was torn between laughter and tears. It wasn't often that a man identified his own shortcomings so succinctly. "It's not your fault," she said. "I threw that at you without any context. I shouldn't have expected a glowing endorsement."

He released her arm, but put a finger alongside her chin and forced her to look at him. "Is that what you were hoping for from me?"

"Maybe. I don't know." The color of his eyes entranced her. The shade reminded her of a summer forest back home. Wriggling away from him, she stood up and wrapped her arms around her waist. "It's not important."

"It must be, or you wouldn't be so upset."

"I'm not upset," she yelled. Stupid man.

He stood up and nodded soberly, though his eyes twinkled. "My apologies for misreading the situation. It might help if you gave me a second chance. I'd really like to hear about this novel of yours."

"We're leaving," she said stubbornly. It was one thing to impulsively mention a lifelong secret dream. It was another entirely to keep plowing ahead when it was obvious the notion of skipping a dissertation was so far out in left field.

Ian wisely allowed the matter to drop, but they were both quiet as they continued their circuit of the island. She suggested a restaurant in the next tiny village. He agreed. The dining room was so small there was no place for a photographer to hide, even if one had gotten wind that Ian was out and about.

A couple of the other patrons shot the lanky Scotsman a curious stare, but their interest could have been attributed to his striking looks instead of anything related to the bachelor list.

The redheaded waitress who brought them their drinks was young and timid. She repeated the dinner order twice. Bella felt sorry for her. Jobs in the area couldn't be thick on the ground. This girl was clearly uncomfortable dealing with the public. Poor thing. Fortunately, she got everything exactly right.

Bella and Ian chatted about this and that while they ate. The changeable Scottish weather. The strength of the dollar against the pound. Whether or not Scotland Yard and the FBI actually had enough personnel to keep tabs on everyone's Internet searches.

Mostly, the conversation was dull as dirt. Bella felt foolish for having lowered her defenses so easily for no other reason than sharing a beautiful blue-skied day with a handsome man. Ian seemed distant now, though he was infinitely polite.

She decided to try one more time. "So tell me, Ian, how can you be away from your work for so long?"

He shrugged, his expression hard to read. "I never use all my vacation days, so I had plenty of time built up for a lengthy sabbatical. Plus, I'm always working in some capacity. As long as I have my laptop with me, I'm never entirely off the grid."

"How do you get your ideas?"

Ian tapped the tines of his fork on the tablecloth, then traced an abstract design. "I could ask you the same thing about your novel. Sometimes it's reading about another scientist's project that jogs my brain. Maybe one day the wisp of an idea simply comes to me. Honestly, I don't really know."

Bella nodded slowly. "I suppose I understand that. I work from imagination, too, though in a different way. I'm always asking myself, 'what if'? And fictional characters live inside my head. I begin to know them. Then I start to write."

His quick grin startled her.

"We're not so different then, are we, lass? Other than coming from opposite sides of the pond and the fact that you are most definitely female and I am not, we both like to see where our brains take us."

"I suppose so," she said slowly. Though in Ian's case, his phenomenal IQ gave him the capacity to truly innovate.

When the little waitress offered dessert, Bella and Ian each declined. Ian smiled at the girl. "We'll take the check now, please."

"Oh, but ye must try the treacle tart. It's the best in all of Scotland." She seemed unduly anxious about the subject.

Bella shook her head. "None for me. Thank you."

Ian nodded. "Nor for me. Another time perhaps." He gave the server a gentle smile that reduced her to silent blushes. But she finally gave up on them.

Unfortunately, she also seemed absurdly slow in returning to the table with their check. The wait was so long Bella finally excused herself and went in search of the facilities. When she exited the bathroom, she had to pass by the corridor that accessed the kitchen.

The ginger-haired waitress was huddled against the wall, her back to Bella. The other woman spoke in a low voice, but Bella could hear every word.

"They're about to leave," the girl whispered. "I can't hold them any longer. If ye want your photograph, ye'd best get here in a hurry."

Bella gaped. Then she charged into action.

Returning to the dining room, she leaned down and whispered in Ian's ear. "Hand me my purse. I have enough cash to cover this. We need to get out of here. Our doe-eyed waitress has ratted you out to the press."

Ian blanched, but refused her offer to pay. He peeled a stack of pound notes from his wallet, tucked them beneath the salt shaker, and followed Bella to the door. Unfortunately, as soon as they peeked out, they saw the very same photographers who had besieged Bella's hilltop home.

Now this was personal. "I saw an exit beside the loo," she said. "Hurry."

Ian didn't waste time arguing. He spun on his heel and followed her, not running, but close. Bella knew she and her dinner companion must look comical to the other diners, but who really cared? Once they sneaked out the back door, they found themselves in an alleyway filled with dust bins. Ian loped to the corner of the building. "The reporters just went inside. We can make it if we hurry."

His legs were longer, but Bella was fueled by righteous indignation. How dare these dweeby little jerks hunt an innocent man like Ian? She jumped into the driver's seat of her brother's Jeep, turned the key in the ignition, and peeled out of the parking lot in a flurry of gravel.

They were only twenty minutes from Portree. Bella kept her foot on the gas aggressively, but with an eye to caution. She didn't want to collide with a hapless sheep.

When she passed town and kept on going, Ian frowned. "Where are we headed?"

"If they follow us back to my place, you're stuck. Everyone will know where you're staying. I've thought of somewhere we can hide out for a couple of hours. The reporters won't be able to find you tonight. They'll give up for the time being, and they still won't be able to prove I'm the one giving you asylum."

Ian's grin, when she glanced sideways to see his reaction, was surprisingly carefree. "Sounds great to me."

* * *

Ian was having fun. It was sobering to realize that even though he enjoyed his life for the most part, rarely could he identify his days as *fun*. Yet with Bella at his side, determined to protect his identity, he felt like a kid again.

Suddenly, she barked out a warning. "Hold on."

Just in time, he grabbed the door handle. The hard left turn as they abruptly exited the main road sent his shoulder banging against the doorframe. *What the hell?* Bella let off on the gas only a fraction in order to maneuver the Jeep over and around dangerous potholes on the rutted, dirt and gravel track.

"Where are we going?" He had to raise his voice to be heard. Though dusk was closing in, there was still plenty of light for anyone following them to spot the Jeep.

"There's a house up here. Deserted. I'll explain in a minute. Do you see anybody on the highway?"

He craned his neck. Far in the distance, from the same direction he and Bella had come, a navy sedan appeared over a rise. Though the car was still a long distance away, it looked like the same one they had seen at the restaurant. "I think that's them. Can you cut the headlights?"

"Good idea."

With the Jeep now running in the near dark, they had to go much slower. Even so, there was little chance the reporters would spot them way up here. The track was steep. As they pulled around behind a small, forlorn cottage and Bella cut the engine, Ian realized they were halfway up the hillside.

In the sudden silence, he could hear his heart beating in his ears. "We'd better get out and see if they're heading our way."

Bella nodded. She tucked her hair behind her ears. "Yes."

She seemed tense, her expression harried.

He put a hand on her forearm. "It's okay," he said. "I can't outrun them forever."

"You shouldn't have to," she said, climbing out of the Jeep. "They're maggots, bottom feeders, scum of the earth."

Ian laughed. "Good Lord, Bella. They're only trying to do their job."

She whirled to face him. "Then why did you run the first time?"

It was a very good question and one he wasn't ready to answer. "Come on," he said. "Let's take a peek."

Carefully, they leaned around the corner of the house and scanned the highway. The navy car was much closer now. Ian held his breath as it pulled even with the wretched, narrow lane and then flew right on by.

Bella exhaled audibly. "Thank goodness."

"We're not out of the woods," he cautioned. "If they think we've given them the slip, they may double back."

"I doubt it. C'mon," she said. "Let's go inside and warm up."

There was a storm on the way, and the air was heavy and moist. "Don't you think it's locked?" he said dubiously. He didn't want to add breaking and entering to his reputation.

Bella laughed softly, the sound hitting him gut deep. "It is. Yes. But I know where the key is hidden."

She was as good as her word. In moments they were inside. Unfortunately, the electricity was not in working order. Ian flipped a switch to no avail. "Now what?"

"We build a fire. We couldn't have turned on the lights anyway, not if we wanted to maintain our hiding place."

"True." He helped her pile logs and rolled-up newspapers in the grate. Unfortunately, the box of matches on the hearth was damp.

After they tried and failed to get a spark three separate times, Bella groaned, rubbing her arms with her hands. "I thought we could hang out here for a few hours and be all cozy. This wasn't part of the plan."

Ian pulled a silver cigarette lighter from his pocket. "This should do the trick," he said.

Bella gaped, her eyes round in the glow of the sudden flames. "You smoke?"

The tone of the question made it sound as if he kicked puppies or stole money from the church.

"I don't," he said mildly. "But if I did, would it be a deal breaker?"

She frowned, sitting down in a rocking chair and pulling her knees up to her chest as if she really were cold. "A deal breaker for what?"

"A deal breaker for us. You and me," he elaborated. In case there was any doubt.

"Umm…"

For once he had stumped the opinionated and prickly southern belle. Ian grabbed the second rocker and angled it to hers, deciding not to push his luck at the moment. He kicked off his shoes and warmed his sock-clad feet on the brass fender. "This is nice. But are you ready to tell me why we're playing squatter in a crofter's cottage in the middle of nowhere?"

Bella recovered her equanimity. "My new sister-in-law, McKenzie, rented this place sight unseen when she came here to spend a month in Scotland. But the owner was old and senile, and when she arrived, the house was in shambles. Finley rescued her until they had a chance to get the cottage cleaned up and in livable condition. It's really a very romantic story."

Ian rocked slowly, extremely conscious of the woman beside him. "So no one lives here now?"

"It's a big secret from McKenzie, but my brother is in the process of purchasing the house from the original owner's family so he can give it to McKenzie as a present on their first anniversary."

"Most men might go with jewelry."

Bella smiled dreamily, her chin resting on her knees. The firelight cast shadows on her face. She looked very young. "You'd have to know McKenzie. She has a great deal of money, but she appreciates simplicity. To have Finley give her this place will please her to no end."

"What would a man have to do to please *you*, Bella? What do you appreciate?"

He saw the muscles in her throat work as she swallowed. "Are you making a pass at me?"

"Does anyone really say that anymore?" There was something very proper and old-fashioned about her wary posture. He found himself flooded with a mixture of tenderness and hunger.

"Okay then," she snapped. "Are you hitting on me?"

He winced. "I'm trying to get to know you." It was the truth, though maybe not the entire truth.

Bella was smart, too smart to be pacified by his equivocation. Still, she didn't pursue her original question. "I like fresh flowers, even in the dead of winter. They make me happy. I adore chocolate, but only in moderation. I enjoy spending time alone. My musical tastes are eclectic. Is that the kind of thing you want to know?"

"It's a start."

"And what about you, Ian Larrimore? What do you do when you're not being hounded by the paparazzi?"

"Nothing very exciting, I assure you. I work and work and work, and when I'm not working, I think about work. I love what I do, so it's difficult to keep my personal life and professional life separate."

"I understand that, I think. Do you run for exercise only, or do you really like it?"

"Both. My chosen field requires a great deal of mental concentration. Getting outside to blow the cobwebs away is not only necessary for good health, but it often gives me a jolt of creative energy. I might be in the middle of a five-mile run and suddenly have a breakthrough."

"That must be exhilarating."

"It is. But what about you? I know from what Finley has told me that you're an academic overachiever. Are you hoping to teach when you finish your dissertation? Mold young minds for the future and all that?"

She wrinkled her nose. "I thought that was what I wanted. Now, I'm not so sure. What I fantasize about is living here in Scotland and spending my days researching history and learning everything I can about the past five hundred years. That's not really a viable life choice, though, so I'm stuck."

"Tell me more about this novel."

"I don't want to talk about it," she said, her expression mulish.

"Why not?"

"Because you're a man and men sneer."

"Says who?"

"Says me."

"Education is supposed to broaden a person's horizons…expand the mind. Why would you make assumptions about me?"

"I've known more than a few 'geniuses' in my academic tenure. Arrogance and intolerance comes with the territory."

"I'm not sure what your brother told you about me, but I assure you I'm neither as intelligent nor as close-minded as you seem to think. I may be a socially awkward introvert, but I'm not a jerk. At least I don't think so."

Chapter Five

Bella realized she was behaving badly. It was possible Ian was making small talk the only way he knew how.

"Will you answer a personal question?" she asked quietly. The time seemed right for shared confidences. Particularly in light of the fact that she had chosen to run interference for this handsome fugitive, not once, but twice.

"I suppose."

"Why does it bother you so much? The attention, I mean. Couldn't you just let them have their photographs and go on your way?"

He scowled. "Why should I *have* to? Is it wrong to want to keep my private life private? I am a human being. A free man. There's something wrong about a society that believes fame obliterates any right to decency and respect."

"You've given this a lot of thought, haven't you?"

He ran both hands through his hair. "I haven't had much choice. The damn cameras are in my face every time I step outside my building. I finally decided I'd had enough. Finley has always given me an open invitation to visit him here on Skye. I called him. He offered me the guest room. End of story. Except for the part where you were in residence. That was a nice surprise."

"Nice? C'mon, Ian. Tell the truth. You were hoping to have the place to yourself. Just like I was."

"Maybe." He took an audible breath. "I'll leave," he said suddenly. "You were here first. It doesn't make sense for you to give up your time in Scotland. You have some big decisions to make."

"Oh, no," she said. "I won't let my brother accuse me of running you off. I'd never live it down. I think we can coexist peacefully if we try."

The room fell silent after that. With the popping and crackling of the fire, Bella grew drowsy. It had been a long day, but she was reluctant to bring up the subject of returning home.

Ian sprawled beside her, his long legs outstretched, his big feet oddly vulnerable. She had a gut feeling he wasn't being honest with her about the paparazzi thing. Yes, it was wrong that one stupid magazine article had turned his world upside down. Still, there had to be more to his reaction than he was admitting.

Lots of celebrities tolerated the limelight by being pleasant and signing autographs on occasion. A man couldn't be chased if he didn't run.

What did Ian have to hide? Was it only his reclusive nature that made him so angry and desperate to elude the reporters hounding his footsteps?

The intimacy of the remote cabin and their darkened hiding place made her jumpy. "I imagine it's safe to go back now, don't you think?"

Ian rested his chin on his chest, his hands laced over his flat belly. She saw his ribcage rise and fall when he sighed. "I suppose." He rolled to his feet and began banking the fire. For good measure they both carried over cups of water and doused the flames. It wouldn't do to burn down Finley's prize.

At last, nothing remained but the smell of damp wood smoke and the lingering sensation of an opportunity missed. Bella felt hollow inside… sad. The emotion made no sense at all. Likely it was the gloom and the late hour creating her melancholy.

She reached into her pocket for the keys to the Jeep and bobbled them, almost tossing them into the hot coals. Fortunately, she managed to catch herself *and* the keys before falling into the arms of Mr. Tall, Geek, and Gorgeous. Too bad.

"You okay?" he asked gruffly.

"I'm fine. Just clumsy." They were standing so close she could inhale the scent of him, memorizing it, dizzy with the notion that she knew it already from some other lifetime. She was not a particularly small woman, but he was big and unequivocally masculine. Her pulse fluttered. "We should probably go now."

He shifted from one foot to the other. "I'm not entirely sure I want to."

His candor shocked her. Why had she ever for a moment believed he was a passive beta male? Having brains didn't preclude the possibility that Ian was the kind of man to *take* what he wanted.

They stood there for an eternity. At last, he reached out and pulled her close, perhaps waiting for her to protest. His chest was comfortingly solid beneath her cheek. His cotton shirt smelled like laundry detergent.

There was no doubt in her mind that she could step away and nothing would happen.

Still, she didn't move.

Ian's hands roved ever so subtly over her lower back, leaving warmth and delight everywhere he touched. "Have I stunned ye, lass?" There was humor in his voice, humor at her expense.

"I thought all you cared about was work," she said. Her hands had fisted at his belt buckle. Now, she slipped her arms around his waist and sighed.

"Don't be daft. I'm a man. You're a woman. And not just any woman," he said quickly. "Ye're bright and funny and cantankerous."

Rude, but accurate, she conceded to herself. "Um, that last one isn't exactly a compliment."

He nuzzled her nose with his. "A bloke likes to work for it sometimes. Ye keep me on my toes. Ye're not a pushover. I like that in a woman."

"To be honest, I'm not always so..."

"Touchy? Prickly? Cranky? Irritable?"

"Enough!" She tried to pinch his waist, but the man didn't have an ounce of flab anywhere on his body. "You bring out the worst in me for some reason."

"Why, Bella?" He stroked her hair with a lazy hand, his fingers winnowing through the strands.

She shrugged. "I'm not exactly sure. I think it has to do with the fact that you're really smart, and you're a man."

"Still not following." The smile in his voice was impossible to miss.

"I've spent most of my life being condescended to because I'm female. *Physics is too hard, Bella. What about art or music? Get your head out of those damned books and go have some fun. I don't think you're exactly what we're looking for in this internship.* My father was the worst, but he wasn't the only one."

"That must have been infuriating. Finley, too?"

"No. Finley is smarter than me, I think, but he never enjoyed school the way I did. He's super proud of me and very supportive."

"What does he think about the dissertation/novel conundrum?"

The room got quiet. They were still standing in front of the fireplace, neither one apparently ready to let go or simply *go*.

"I haven't told him about the novel," she said, her words barely audible.

"Why not?"

"Well, there was the wedding and all that..."

"Excuses, excuses."

"Don't be mean. I know what he'll say."

"And that is?"

"He'll tell me to follow my dreams or something syrupy sweet like that."

"I've known Finley for some time now. The last thing I would ever call him is *sweet*."

She chuckled. "Fair point. But he does have a soft spot when it comes to me. He feels guilty, because when he moved here to Skye a decade ago, he left me to handle our father. That was no easy task."

"If you're positive Finley will be supportive, what's so scary about broaching the subject of your dissertation with him?"

"Why must you be so infuriatingly logical?" she muttered. "Some things come from the gut and aren't easy to explain."

"Try me."

His insistence made their present posture uncomfortable. Instead of elaborating, she pulled away and rubbed her arms. "I'd like to go back to the house now." She didn't really want to pull away. Ian Larrimore was a very wonderful human to cozy up to…in all sorts of tantalizing ways. Even so, she didn't need a man to fix her problems.

"Bella—"

She held up a hand when he tried to touch her. "No. Seriously, Ian. It's time to leave."

The small cottage was dark. The rain and wind had moved in, drummed on the roof for an hour, and moved on. Ian moved restlessly. "I suppose you're right." He didn't sound too happy about it.

When they were outside and the door safely locked behind them, he put himself between her and the Jeep. "What are you doing?" she asked.

"Wouldn't you like me to drive? This lane is a suicide course, especially in the dark."

"You don't trust me?"

His low curse surprised her. "For God's sake, Bella. I thought you might be tired. Forgive me for being a gentleman. Hell, I think I'll walk. It's the only thing that will keep me from strangling you."

Before she could say a word, he took off on foot, striding down the hill at a breakneck pace. "Wait," she cried. "It's a long way. I'm sorry."

Either he didn't hear her or he was too angry to stop.

Muttering beneath her breath, she jumped into the Jeep and started the engine. Or tried to. The motor gave a wheezing sound and died. "No, no, no…" she cried. When she cranked the ignition a second time, the engine didn't respond at all.

Swallowing her pride was the only option. She was good at a lot of things, but auto mechanics was not one of them.

Ian had long legs, and he was in his physical prime. Though she jogged down the hill, it took her several minutes to find him. He was sitting on a rock, his elbows on his knees.

"Where's the Jeep?" he asked, his tone mildly conversational.

"Where do you think?" She clapped her hand over her mouth. Ian was right. She *was* cranky. "I'm sorry," she said quickly. "It's still up behind the house. I couldn't get it started. Why are you sitting here?"

He stood and brushed off his pants. "When you didn't pass me, I started to wonder what had happened to you."

"I'm fine. We might have to walk back to Portree, though. The Jeep is deader than dead."

"Let me take a look at it."

Less than an hour ago, Bella had been in Ian's arms waiting for a kiss that never came. Now they trudged back up the hill in silence, together, but apart. Not exactly the most romantic evening Bella had ever spent with a man, but not the worst, either. She and Ian were the proverbial oil and water. In spite of that fact, or perhaps because of it, she found him stimulating in more ways than one.

The lane was steep. Bella tried to keep her huffing and puffing to a minimum, so Ian wouldn't judge. She wasn't a slug; she exercised. Sometimes. Her companion, on the other hand, strode along as if enjoying a walk in the park. It was demoralizing and inexplicable. For a brainiac who spent his days focused on cerebral matters, the man was a remarkable physical specimen.

Disaster lurked in the darkness. Bella didn't see one of the small potholes and went down hard on her left foot. Her ankle twisted awkwardly and pain shot up her leg as she collapsed in an ungainly heap.

When she yelped, Ian stopped immediately and crouched beside her. "Don't move," he said. "Ye don't want to make it worse."

"Thank you, *Doctor* Larrimore." The sarcasm was instinctive, although in hindsight, she realized he probably *did* have a doctorate, rendering the insult somewhat moot.

He brushed a strand of hair from her cheek. "Finley talks about you like you're an angel. The man must be blinded by fraternal devotion. Ye've a mouth like a heider."

"A heider?" Sometimes with his accent she wasn't sure she understood the words.

"Aye. A heider...a crazy person. I never know what ye'll come up with next."

"Can you quit haranguing me long enough to look at my ankle, please?"

He didn't answer. Instead, he gently lifted her leg out of the hole and rested her ankle in his hand. "I left my phone in the Jeep. Can ye shine the light from yours?"

Bella fumbled in her pocket, trying to keep movement to a minimum. The pain made her nauseated. When she managed to engage the flashlight app, she groaned. Ian probed gently, but even his light touch was agonizing. Her foot had swollen visibly already.

He removed her sock and shoe. "We've got to get you back," he said calmly. "We'll need ice and painkillers."

"It's not that bad," Bella protested.

He lifted her chin with a finger, forcing her to look at him. "Out of curiosity, if I were to say the sky is blue, would you disagree?"

"Is that supposed to be funny?"

"Not at all. I'm merely trying to gauge the depth of your commitment to contrarianism."

"That's not a real thing."

He helped her to her feet, supporting her with one hand. "Of course it is. I'm going to turn around now. Do you think you can get up on my back? Put your arms around my neck and balance on one foot."

"I'm not a child. I can figure this out."

When she stumbled and bumped her injured foot, she uttered an unladylike but very appropriate word. Ian was silent, but his shoulders shook, so she was pretty sure he was laughing at her. *Beast.*

Riding piggyback on a man was a very intimate thing to do. It was also mortifying. "I'm too heavy," she said when she finally heaved herself onto him.

Ian reached behind and put his hands under her thighs. "Don't be ridiculous. Ye're little more than a sprite."

Nevertheless, he grunted when he hefted her bottom a few inches higher and set off up the track. "I could probably walk," she said. "If you put me down."

Her Sherpa kept a steady pace. "I've run two marathons this year," he said. "I think I can manage you."

"Aren't you a little big for a serious runner?"

His chuckle sounded strained. "All the men in my father's family are tall and broad. It's genetics, ye know. My ancestors carried boulders from place to place. Sturdy stock."

When they at last reached the Jeep, Ian set her down gently. She leaned against the vehicle, balancing on one foot. He opened the door and helped her into the backseat so she could stretch out.

"Do you need me to hold things?" she asked suddenly, uncomfortable with her role as maiden in distress.

Leaning in, he captured her chin, found her mouth, and kissed her lazily. *Oh, wow.* The man knew a thing or two about kissing. When he was done, they were both breathless. He backed out of the Jeep and straightened. "I'll no' be needing you to hold anything, lass. At least not now. Quit distracting me, so I can get us back on the road."

After that he raised the hood and she lost sight of him. Amidst the banging and male muttering, she zoned out for a moment. With her fingers on her lips, she tried to recall the breathless seconds when Ian staked a claim. The recollection made her dizzy. Although to be honest, that might be because her ankle hurt like all the devils of hell were stomping on it.

"Ian," she called out. "Do you know what's wrong?"

He appeared at her side, holding something in his hand. "I think 'twas probably the heavy rain. The alternator cap is loose. Damp inside. We'll need to leave it open for a bit to dry things out. Then I'll try the engine again."

"Okay." She shivered. How long would they have to stay in the depressing, chilly dark?

Ian put the cap on the floorboard at her feet and shrugged out of his shirt. "Here. Sit up so I can put this on you. I don't want to risk you going into shock."

"I'm fine," she protested automatically, but she had to admit the delicious lingering warmth from his body heat was wonderfully comforting. Ian had been wearing a thin, long sleeve striped shirt unbuttoned over a thicker traditional tee. Now he had only the tee. "Won't you be cold now?" she asked.

He brushed his thumb across her cheek. "If I get too cold, I'll just ask for another kiss."

"You didn't ask for the first one," she called out indignantly as he walked away again.

His only response was laughter.

Fortunately, Ian's knowledge of the internal combustion engine proved sufficient to get the Jeep going again. When the motor turned over and purred normally, Bella sighed. "Thank goodness."

Ian sat in the driver's seat. He flipped on the overhead light and turned to look at her. "Shall I drive?" he asked, his expression deadpan.

He was baiting her, pure and simple. Unwilling to be bested in a war of words, she pursed her lips and furrowed her brow to let him know she was thinking deeply. "Well, it *is* my left foot that's damaged, so I should be able to get us back in one piece."

Her statement was patently absurd. Ian gaped, incredulity in his gaze. "Are you serious?"

"Of course not, you big egghead." She punched his shoulder. "Let's go home. I'm inclined to let you pamper me for at least twenty-four hours."

Ian turned back to the wheel and put the Jeep in gear. "God help us all," he muttered.

Chapter Six

Ian knew he was wading into deep waters. One kiss and his IQ had dropped at least forty points. Fortunately, the effect was temporary. As long as he kept his distance, he probably wouldn't do something stupid.

There were any number of valid reasons not to get involved with Bella Craig. First of all, she was Finley's sister. Brothers tended to take those kinds of relationships very seriously. For Ian to even think about being intimate with the lovely Bella would be enough to give his friend a coronary.

Secondly, Ian sucked at relationships. He loved sex. And he'd had no complaints from the few women he'd dabbled with since earning his final degree and striking out on his own. When it came to daily interaction, though, that's where things fell apart.

Ian tended to have laser focus when he was working. More than one woman had told him she didn't appreciate being ignored for long stretches of time. Bella would be harder to ignore than most, but it could happen. Then her feelings would be hurt. She would call him a jerk and a loser, and it would be over.

Oddly enough, he enjoyed sparring with her almost as much as he might revel in sharing her bed. Almost, but not quite. Still, the prospect of terminating this budding friendship sobered him. Maybe given the circumstances, he should enjoy her company and keep a lid on his baser instincts.

Bella was vulnerable. Strong and capable, but vulnerable. Men had undervalued her time and again, leaving her wary and combative. He didn't want to be responsible for adding another layer to her armor.

She didn't speak during the drive back to town, and neither did he. When they made it back to Finley's house, Ian could hear Cinnamon barking a welcome inside. Anytime Bella planned to be gone for the day, she hired a teenager from the village to walk and feed the dog.

Ian shut off the engine and hopped out, prepared for battle. He opened her door. "You'll have to let me carry you. If you're on your feet when we go inside, that crazy dog will knock you down."

"Okay." In the illumination from the small bulb of the porch light, he could see that Bella suffered. Her face was pale as milk. She clenched her jaw when he leaned in to scoop her up.

He had expected a fight. The fact that she curled her arm around his neck without protest and rested her head against his chest worried him. "Maybe we should go straight to the hospital," he muttered, torn between wanting to get her comfortable quickly and the possibility the ankle might be broken.

At last Bella put her foot down, metaphorically speaking. "No hospital," she said. "Not for a sprain. If I can't put weight on it in forty-eight hours, then I'll go."

"Do you have any idea if Finley owns a pair of crutches?"

"Actually, he does. From a motorcycle wreck he had a few years ago. I saw them in the hall closet on the landing."

"Good. Rest and more rest tonight, but knowing you, you'll need them tomorrow."

"I'm not stupid," she said, her voice subdued. "I'll behave."

The entirely inappropriate mental image of *making* Bella behave gave him a very inconvenient boner. Enough that he stumbled on the top step. "Sorry," he muttered. He fished out the key his hostess had provided and unlocked the front door. Cinnamon bounded against his legs, almost sending both humans crashing to the floor. "Easy, girl," he said. "We're glad to see you, too. But the lady of the house is hurt. You'll have to help me make sure she's okay." He could swear the dog understood every word.

The trek up the stairs past his room and on up to the next floor was slow but uneventful. Bella made a quick visit to the en suite with his assistance as far as the door, and then he tucked her into bed. While in the bathroom, she had changed into a lemon yellow T-shirt and cotton drawstring bottoms in navy with tiny yellow palm trees all over them.

He made her lie back so he could examine her injury. With better lighting, her ankle looked far worse. Puffy and bruised, it was a mess. "I'm wondering if I should wrap it," he mused aloud.

"Oh no," she pleaded. "I don't even know if I can bear to have the sheet touch it."

"So putting on those pajama pants must have hurt like hell. Why didn't you let me help?"

Her eyes widened. "Because you would have seen my underwear."

He grinned. "Leopard print bikinis? Satiny pink thong? Black lace see-through?"

"Don't be ridiculous." Her face was red from her throat to her hairline. He loved the way she got all hot and bothered when he teased her. Just like the Banty hens his grand-da used to raise.

He decided to take pity on her. "Shall I forage in the medicine cabinet and see what I can find?"

She nodded carefully, her blue eyes dull with fatigue and discomfort. "I saw a prescription bottle in there, but I didn't pay attention."

Fortunately, the tablets were a strong pain reliever left over from Finley's crash. He examined the bottle with a frown. "This says to take two every four to six hours, but you're a lot smaller than your brother. What if we try half of one? If that's enough for you to rest comfortably, it would be better to err on the side of caution."

"Makes sense. But I'll need a small snack if you don't mind. Crackers maybe. I don't want to upset my stomach. And Ian..." She raised up on one elbow, her expression agitated.

"What?" He rested his forearm against the doorway to the hall, keeping his distance. That was the plan.

"You're not responsible for me. I really appreciate your help, but after I take this pill, you're off the clock. Go to sleep or to work or whatever, but don't think you have to check up on me. I'll be fine."

"What if I *want* to check up on you?" he asked mildly. Her insistence on shoving him out the door sparked his temper.

"Why would you? I'm an adult capable of caring for myself. You're Finley's guest."

"Lord, you're a piece of work. We're sharing a house, Bella. We enjoyed a perfectly lovely day together right up until the moment those damned reporters showed up. You've hurt yourself, and I'm right here under your roof. What's the big deal?"

She went paler still, if that were possible. "I don't like relying on other people."

It was probably the most honest thing she had said to him thus far. "I'm not infringing on your independence, Bella. The world is a better place when people are kind to each other. Where's the harm in that?"

"I don't want you to be kind to me," she said, the words barely audible. "I'd really rather you tear off my clothes and ravish me."

Ian was almost positive his heart stopped beating for a full ten seconds. His throat dried and his skin felt clammy. Maybe *he* was the one in shock. "I don't think that would be a very good idea."

"Why not?" She turned on her side, the side without the damaged ankle, and tucked her hand beneath her cheek. Big blue eyes stared at him without blinking.

He coughed. "You're not serious. You just like getting men to dance around like damned puppets. I won't be manipulated by sex."

"Methinks thou doth protest too much."

The little witch was getting to him. "I'm going to fetch you something to eat," he said formally. "I won't be long."

In the kitchen he opened the freezer and stuck his head inside. Was it possible for a man his age to have a massive coronary? He was shaky and weak, and he could hear his heart pounding in his ears. Never in his life had he wanted a woman so badly.

Bella was joking. That much was clear. In her condition, nothing would happen even if she *weren't* taunting him. She was injured, in pain, and out of control...all valid reasons why a woman like her would try to get the upper hand by teasing him.

His analytical brain sorted through the explanation with concise precision. The resultant conclusion did nothing at all to curb his libido. Proximity and what he believed to be a mutual attraction threatened to do him in....

Thank God for sprained ankles. It was the only thing keeping him from losing more IQ points before morning came.

When he returned to the master bedroom, Bella's eyes were closed. In Finley's big king-sized bed she looked defenseless and harmless. Both impressions were false. He'd never met a woman more capable of holding her own with the opposite sex.

While she dozed, he catalogued the contents of the room, giving himself breathing space to handle the next round with his unpredictable sparring partner. Finley's bedroom was sparsely furnished and gave off a definite masculine vibe. The new bride had added a few touches here and there, but for the most part, this was a man's hideaway.

No doubt, there would be remodeling done soon. Or perhaps Finley would sell the quirky cottage. That thought saddened Ian. He had always admired the man who crossed an ocean and created the life he wanted. Granted, Finley had been running from something...or someone. Bella and Finley's father was a hard man by all accounts.

Still, Finley had found himself here in the Scottish Highlands. The motorcycles he built by hand were works of art. The rich and famous came from around the globe to purchase them. Ian had always pitied celebrities and their hemmed-in existence. Now by a quirk of fate, he resembled one in a very minor way.

He must have made a noise, because Bella's eyes opened drowsily. "Sorry," she said. "I didn't mean to fall asleep."

"Long day," he said.

"Yes."

Avoiding eye contact, he approached the bed and held out a small plate of buttered crackers and a glass of milk. "This will have to do, I'm afraid. Nothing else in the kitchen looked appetizing at this hour."

She sat up and shoved the hair from her face, wincing when her foot protested. "It's fine. I'm not really hungry."

While he broke a pill in half, Bella ate three crackers and drank most of the milk. When he handed her the medicine, their fingers brushed. "I hope this works," he said.

"Thank you."

Clearly, the pain was making an impact. That, and fatigue. There was no hint of mischief in Bella's face now, no teasing repartee. He told himself he was glad. Not that he wanted her to be hurt. But a subdued Bella was less dangerous.

At last she offered him the empty plate and glass. "I'm sure I'll sleep now. I appreciate your help."

He shrugged. "You made sure we eluded the reporters at the restaurant. I owe you one for that."

"Then we'll call it even. Good night, Ian."

"Leave your door unlocked. If you fall in the night, I'll need to get to you."

"What makes you think I'll fall?"

"Have you ever walked on crutches before?"

"No. Have you?"

"Actually, yes. More than once. The last time was after hamstring surgery. I'll tell you from experience that it makes more sense to follow the doctor's orders from the beginning rather than risk further injury."

"Duly noted."

"Okay then. Good night." Why were his feet not moving? Perhaps it was the way her soft T-shirt clung to her breasts. Or the unfathomable mysteries hidden in deep blue eyes. What was she thinking?

He didn't have to wonder for long. She waved a hand. "Go. I promise I won't bother you in the middle of the night."

Nodding tersely, he left the room and shut the door, knowing that her words were a lie. She *would* bother him in the middle of the night. Everything about Bella Craig bothered him.

The question was, what was he going to do about it?

* * *

The following morning, Bella awoke at dawn with her stomach growling and her body aching. Apparently, when she twisted her ankle, she had wrenched other muscles as well. She felt like an old lady.

Ordinarily, she would go for an immediate cup of coffee, but since she had a guest in the house, she was forced to at least wash her face and brush her hair. The long waves were wild from the damp air last night, so she caught them up in a loose ponytail. After that, she slicked gloss over her lips. Seconds later, she rubbed it off with a tissue and glared at her reflection in the mirror.

It didn't matter one little bit what she looked like at this hour in the morning. Ian Larrimore was no more than an inconvenience to her. Period.

Trying to use two crutches to negotiate the multi-level house seemed hazardous, so she tucked one crutch under her arm and set out. Fortunately, the short, crooked flights of stairs at least had sturdy handrails. Moving slowly, she made her way to the kitchen. Cinnamon looked up, alert and happy, when Bella hobbled into the room. Surprisingly, the dog stayed put. She had obviously taken Ian's lecture to heart.

"Hello, sweetheart. Sorry I can't get down and play with you today. I'll make it up to you when I can walk again."

The dog's tongue lolled. Her tail swished briskly.

Bella sighed as she poured her coffee, noting that someone in the house had been up early. "I know you miss Finley. I miss him, too. And McKenzie. I've never had a sister. I hope she and I can be friends."

Cinnamon's silent encouragement was surprisingly comforting.

"The thing is," Bella said, sitting down at the table and nursing her drink, "I've lost my way. Does that make sense? I thought I had my whole life mapped out in advance. Now I'm not so sure. Look at Finley. He was practically a confirmed bachelor. Then *kaboom*. He runs into McKenzie on a dark road, and a romance is born."

Cinnamon rested her nose on her tail and whined.

"I know what you're thinking," Bella said. "Finley's older than I am and ready to settle down. He didn't know that, though, did he? Until he met McKenzie, all he wanted to do was build motorcycles."

The one-sided conversation might have continued, but someone knocked at the front door. Bella glanced at the clock and then at her attire. It was early for visitors. When she peeked out the curtains in the living room, she smiled and opened the door. "Hilda! What's up?"

The other woman cocked her head and studied the crutch. "I think that's my question, lass. Ye don't look so well. May I come in?"

"Of course." Once they were both settled, Bella indicated her foot. "I twisted my ankle yesterday. I don't think anything is broken. Shouldn't you be opening up the store?"

Hilda and her husband owned an upscale gift shop in the village. Hebridean jewelry. Beautiful pottery. Matted photographs. It was mostly a seasonal business, but they managed to squeak by in the lean months. She and Bella had met each other on one of Bella's earlier visits to Skye, and the friendship stuck.

Hilda set a small paper-wrapped parcel on the coffee table. "I made you a loaf of my pumpernickel bread. My mother-in-law has the children today. She's taking them to Inverness to buy new shoes. It makes her happy and gives me a break. Not to mention my dear husband thinks we're going to close up shop for the lunch hour and canoodle. He's a randy old fool, and I've told him so."

Despite the complaint, the other woman radiated smug happiness that only someone in an intimate relationship could display.

Bella smiled wistfully. Hilda's boys were three and almost five, the image of their father but with Hilda's freckles and sly humor. "I'm always up for company. Still, why are you here when you could be reading a book with your feet up?"

The wiry Scotswoman was little more than thirty-five, but she seemed older. She leaned forward with a conspiratorial smile. "I thought I'd ask ye face to face."

"Ask me what?"

"Is he really here? Is he staying with you?"

"Umm…" Bella leaned forward to rub her ankle, giving herself a moment to think, searching frantically for the right answer. She had managed to fool the press when Ian first arrived, but Hilda wouldn't be fobbed off with a half-truth.

Hilda sat back and stared, her jaw slack, her expression wide-eyed. "So it's true then. He's here."

"Who are you talking about?"

"Don't be coy, missy. Ye're playing house with the second most eligible bachelor in all the UK, aren't you?"

Bella whispered a vague, desperate prayer. *Please don't let Ian walk in.* Surely he would hear that Bella had a visitor and keep his distance.

"Why on earth would you think that, Hilda? Do you really believe Cinnamon would let a strange man in the house?"

"Don't try to fool me. Everyone in town is talking about it. I thought surely you would have told me if it was true."

Bella's heart sank. This woman was her friend. In Hilda's eyes she saw disappointment and hurt. "Hilda…" She trailed off, trying to solve the conundrum. "Sometimes a woman has to make difficult choices to honor a promise. Do you understand what I'm saying?"

Hilda's brow furrowed. "Ye've made a promise? To whom?"

Bella remained silent, giving her visitor time to sort through the equivocation.

Suddenly, the Scotswoman's face cleared. "Ye've promised the man ye won't divulge his location."

"My brother has lots of friends." Again, a non sequitur that might explain without elaboration.

Hilda was sharp. She cocked her head. "Finley told this Ian fellow he could hide out here. Ye're complicit in the scheme. Have I got it?"

"Nice weather we're having today, isn't it?" Bella grinned.

"Ach, lass, ye're a sly one. Now when I'm out and about, if anyone asks me what I know, I'll simply tell them there's no evidence at all that the famous Mr. Larrimore is anywhere near the vicinity of Portree."

Bella nodded slowly. "Tell me what's new at the shop," she said.

Despite her understanding, Hilda was clearly disappointed. As Bella's friend, she obviously had hoped for an inside track to an encounter with Britain's second most eligible bachelor.

Chapter Seven

After the two of them chatted for almost an hour, Bella began to get antsy. The two cups of coffee she had drunk were making themselves known. Bella couldn't risk leaving Hilda unattended while Bella made a trip to the bathroom. What was she going to do?

Fortunately, Hilda's long-suffering husband called her cell phone to say a tour bus had unloaded on the street and he needed Hilda's help with the shoppers. At last, the other woman stood. "I'd best be gettin' down the hill or he'll accuse me of bletherin' all day while he's hard at work."

"You don't fool me. That man dotes on you."

Hilda preened. "Aye, 'tis true."

Bella got up with her single crutch, said good-bye to her friend, and locked the door behind Hilda. Not everyone in these parts was security conscious, but with reporters likely still nearby, Bella erred on the side of caution. She didn't want unexpected company, especially not the kind who might slip in without permission.

After a quick trip to the loo, she managed the steps to the landing where the guest room was situated. Wrinkling her nose in indecision, she knocked lightly on Ian's door. "Ian, she's gone. You can come out now." No answer. Well shoot. Was he ignoring her deliberately?

As much as she enjoyed Hilda's company, she couldn't help thinking about last night and all that had happened. The pleasant dinner, the blood-pumping escape from the paparazzi, the cozy time by the fire in the cabin, her twisted ankle. And then the kiss…

The kiss. It was either a beginning or an unfortunate slip. Sadly, she concluded it was the latter. Flirting with Ian was fun. That's all it was. He would only be hiding out from the press for a short while. Probably about the time Ian returned to London, Bella would be on her way to the

Orkneys for a few days. It was a trip she had planned weeks ago. Her house-sitting duties would be covered while she was gone by the same teenager who looked after Cinnamon now and again.

The prospect of that upcoming adventure had beckoned on the horizon like the cherry on the top of her wonderful visit to Scotland. Why now had it lost its luster?

With the *step-clunk* that was her new less than graceful pattern, she climbed another flight of stairs and made it to her bedroom. This walking-with-crutches thing was not easy.

It took more effort than it should to shower, wash and dry her hair, and dress in loose-fitting black knit pants and a soft jersey top. The shirt was peony pink. She needed the bright color to boost her mood.

Nothing had changed. With Finley on his honeymoon, she had an unprecedented and extremely affordable opportunity to explore the country that had intrigued her for years. Ian was not part of the equation. He was a blip on the radar. An annoying fly on the windshield of her life.

Unfortunately, no amount of rationalization could take away the feeling that she was missing out on something wonderful.

When she went downstairs for lunch, she found evidence that Ian had already eaten. That fact shouldn't have hurt. It was a sandwich and a drink. Ian had told her he focused intensely when he was working. Likely he didn't want to be interrupted while his impressive brain was calculating obscure equations with multiple variables.

Moodily, she sat at the kitchen table—solo—and consumed an apple with peanut butter. Not even Cinnamon was around to keep her company. The goofy dog was probably holed up with Ian in the guest room.

Suddenly, Bella couldn't stand being cooped up in the house a minute longer. Using both crutches this time, she retrieved her purse and a small backpack and set out for Eilean Donan Castle. It wasn't terribly far… across the new bridge and on around toward Dornie.

Only when she arrived and the ticket seller apologetically explained that the tour was not handicap friendly because of all the uneven stairs and narrow corridors, did Bella realize that her injury was going to hinder her ability to explore. Instead of touring the picturesque home of the MacRaes, she could only enjoy the grounds.

As second best, it wasn't a bad option. The castle sat on a tiny island where three great lochs converged. Though the original structure had been destroyed and rebuilt several times over the centuries, its latest facelift in the early years of the twentieth century had restored the castle to its former glory. A stone bridge encouraged visitors to approach and admire.

Although it was awkward, Bella managed to balance on one crutch and take photographs with her iPhone. Eilean Donan was striking from any angle. With the clouds and the water, and the wind whipping the Scottish flag, it wasn't hard to see why this particular location had been used repeatedly in television and movies. The massive stone castle was impressive. It conjured up images of centuries long gone by.

All the wonderful photographs in the world didn't make up for the fact that she wanted to see what was inside. Another day. Maybe even another trip. Her time in Scotland was speeding by much faster than she had anticipated. Not that she couldn't visit Finley again in the future, but she was surprised by how quickly the days were ticking off on the calendar.

Because her ankle was aching, she bought a cinnamon scone in the bustling visitor center café and sat down to eat it, her swollen foot propped on a chair. Clearly, she had endured enough physical activity for one day. No point in making things worse.

The pain and swelling had stabilized, though, so she didn't see the need for X-rays. She'd always heard that bad sprains took longer to heal than breaks. Patience was all she required, not medical care.

As she enjoyed the pastry, she acknowledged the truth. She didn't want to go back to Finley's house. She was afraid Ian would be there, and she was afraid he *wouldn't* be there. How did her perfect sabbatical get messed up so quickly? It was ridiculous to feel exiled from her own house.

The snack wasn't going to hold her for long. On the way back, she decided to stop in town and order chicken cacciatore for two. If Ian was MIA, she would simply save the other half for her lunch tomorrow.

By the time an hour and a half elapsed, she had developed a great appreciation for people with mobility issues. Parking, walking to the restaurant, carrying the food to the car—all while on crutches—was hard.

At last, she made it back to her home away from home. She felt hot and grubby and out of sorts. Somehow, all her frustrations led back to Ian. She couldn't blame the injured ankle on him. That was her own carelessness, but dreading the thought of going inside was all his fault.

She could hear Cinnamon barking. If Finley was home, he had to know she was back. No sooner had she made it up the steps than Ian jerked open the door. She had her hand on the knob, so she nearly overbalanced. He rescued the food just in time and put his arm around her waist.

"Sorry," he muttered. "I didn't mean to make it worse."

Ian was fresh out of the shower. His thick chestnut hair was damp and his tanned skin smelled like manly soap. Bella might have swooned, but she didn't trust the darn crutches to hold her up. She tried to wiggle free.

"I'm all sweaty," she said. "Let me go."

He dropped a kiss on her nose but released her. "I thought I might have to send out search and rescue. I had no idea where you were. For all I knew, you might have tripped and fallen down a hill."

"Your concern is touching. I might point out, though, that if you hadn't been sneaking around like a ghost earlier today, I could have told you my plans. Where were you, anyway?"

He led the way to the kitchen and set the bag on the table, sniffing appreciatively. "Smells wonderful." He grabbed a bottle of wine from the fridge and started peeling back the foil around the cork. "When I realized you had company, I spent some time in Finley's workshop. If I had stayed in my room, your friend would have heard the floors creak. I didn't want to make things awkward for you."

Bella scowled, but it was halfhearted at best. "Well, if that was your concern, you should have stayed in London," she muttered.

Ian handed her a chilled glass of chardonnay. "Not nice, Bella. Not nice at all. What would Finley say?"

She took a long slug of wine and sighed. "Finley can go stuff it. I never signed on to be an innkeeper."

"Someone's in a pleasant mood," Ian said, eyeing her over the rim of his glass. His steady regard made her squirm.

"For once, it's not your fault. I went to tour Eilean Donan Castle this afternoon. It's been on my to-do list forever, but it didn't occur to me that medieval castles aren't retrofitted for crutches and wheelchairs. I looked rather foolish, if you must know. I think the guy who wouldn't sell me a ticket felt sorry for me."

"Poor Bella. I'll take you back when you can walk again, I promise."

"How long exactly are you planning to stay?" The question came out more sharply than she intended. The uncertainty of their cohabitation situation made her ill at ease.

Instead of answering, Ian carefully set down his glass of wine, fetched a couple of plates from the cabinet, and began putting the food out on the table. When Bella tried to stand and help, he shot her a hot, irritated glance. "For God's sake, sit down. I've got this. If you so much as move a muscle, I'll tie you to that chair."

And just like that, the specter of intimacy appeared again.

Bella looked down at her food, her heart racing. She was afraid to pick up her fork, because her hand was trembling, and she didn't want him to see.

The silence after his heated rebuke lasted for twelve and a half minutes.

She knew, because she tracked the awkward void on the kitchen clock. Little by little she forced herself to take bites, but the food stuck in her throat.

Ian ate quickly, either because he was starving or because he wanted to get away from her and back to his computer. Was she imagining his sexual subtext? It wasn't a skill she'd ever excelled at…gauging a man's interest.

When she had eaten enough to make it look as though everything was normal, she poked at the remainder with her fork. "Did you have a productive day?"

Ian looked at her, his eyebrow raised. "Small talk? Really? Are we having afternoon tea? Should I extend my pinkie finger?"

"Don't be a sarcastic ass."

"It's the only kind of ass I know."

The droll comment made her laugh, and oddly enough unraveled the knot in her stomach. "What exactly is it that you do?" She couldn't believe they had shared a roof for several days now and she still didn't know.

He shrugged. "It's hard to explain."

"'Cause I'm not as smart as you?"

For a moment she thought he was going to jam his fork, tines down, in Finley's old-fashioned, already scarred oak table. "You have to be the most impossible, *contermacious* woman I've ever met."

"You're not exactly easy, now are you? Go ahead. Try me. Tell me about a day in the life of Ian Larrimore." She wasn't familiar with that Scottish adjective he used, but from the context, she could guess.

He rubbed two fingers in the center of his forehead. "I'm part of an experimental think tank. We're funded by a handful of nonprofits and charged with creating ways to make the world a safer and better place."

"We?"

"There are nine of us. Each with his or her own specialty. We brainstorm together twice a month, but when we have an idea, we run with it on an individual basis. Most of us are not comfortable with creation by committee, though we've come to learn that there really is something to the idea that two heads are better than one."

"I'm impressed."

"Sarcasm?" He lifted an eyebrow.

"Not at all. You're the first person I've ever known who works in a fish tank."

"Think tank."

"Oh, right. I forgot."

"I see the problem," he said suddenly, his gaze holding hers like a mesmerist.

"Problem?"

"You said men don't like it because you're so smart."

"I never said exactly that."

"But it's true, right?"

"Um...yes. I suppose."

"You must talk circles around them...the poor clueless ones, I mean. They don't stand a chance."

"I like interesting conversation. What's wrong with that?"

Now he focused his gaze on her mouth. It might have been her chin, but she was almost certain it was her lips. She bit the bottom one to keep it from trembling. "Quit staring."

"Utterly impossible," he said quietly. "You are a stunning woman."

"Until I open my mouth. That's what most people think. I tried being quiet and ladylike once, but it didn't take."

"Do I make you nervous, Bella?"

His wicked smile slid beneath her defenses and made her want things that were unwise. "Of course not," she lied.

He reached out and took her hands in his. "Tell me about your novel," he coaxed. "I'd love to hear about it. Truly."

A lump in her throat made it difficult to speak. His gaze was warm and charming. Honest. Was he truly interested, or was this a ploy to win her trust? "I don't want to."

"Please." He squeezed her fingers, conveying an intimacy she needed so badly it scared her.

She pulled away, wanting to stand up, but hampered by her injured foot. The only way to put distance between them was to fold her arms over her chest. "It's hard to explain."

"Now where have I heard that before?" he teased gently.

"Oh. Sorry." She had called him out for using that same excuse. "Well, it's probably a longshot. There are a million people out there writing books these days."

"But they don't have your brains and your passion for the time period."

"Some of them do..."

"Bella..." The warning note in his voice told her it was time to come clean about her secret project.

"I've been working on a massive outline for ages. It's going to be historical fiction with a strong romantic element."

"Go on. Tell me more."

"My main character is a commoner who bears the bastard child of a nobleman. She knows her only chance out of poverty and obscurity is to convince her lover that the son is brilliant and needs to be part of court somehow. Basically, she makes sure that the nobleman falls in love with his child. She doesn't allow him to ignore the boy, so gradually a bond forms."

"Fascinating."

Bella searched his face. His comment appeared to be genuine. Still, it was difficult for her to take it at face value. "That's all I've come up with so far," she said abruptly. "You probably have work to do. I need to rest."

Ian sat back in his chair and leaned it on two hind legs. "Why do you do that?"

"Do what?" She held herself tighter as if the kitchen were chilly, when in fact, it was delightfully cozy.

"Whenever we make progress, you shove me away."

"What does that mean...*progress*?"

"Now who's being clueless? I like you, Bella. And I think you like me."

"You're not bad," she said grudgingly.

"Damned with faint praise." His smile made her want to climb across the table and curl into his lap. "I understand the word no. If you're not interested in pursuing this attraction, all you have to do is say so."

She gaped. "Attraction?"

He nodded solemnly. "You remember that thing you said about ravishing me?"

"That was the drugs talking. Besides, you were supposed to ravish *me,* not the other way around."

"You said it *before* I gave you the drugs. And since I know how you feel about gender stereotypes, I'm happy to play your submissive if that's something you want."

"Submissive?" She looked at him in horror, no less shocked than if he had sprouted horns and tail feathers.

"I've never had a woman tie me up. It might be fun."

"It wouldn't. Be fun," Bella clarified. "I'm not good at that kind of stuff. I've never *done* those things," she clarified. "I think we got off track somehow. We were talking about my novel."

"The one where the nobleman has a beautiful and enthusiastic mistress? I remember."

"I never said she was enthusiastic."

"If the nobleman was handsome and wealthy, I'm sure she was enthusiastic."

Chapter Eight

It was no easy task, but Ian had finally gotten the upper hand. At least for the moment. It was a damn good feeling. His working group in London included four unique women. They were all highly educated and very smart, but none of them had Bella's extraordinary combination of intellect, wit, and charm.

She would lead some man a merry dance someday.

Oddly, the thought of Bella getting married disturbed him. It would take a special man to live up to her challenging personality. She was brilliant, intuitive, and actually had the people skills so many advanced minds lacked. It would be a crime for her to end up with a guy who didn't appreciate her unusual range of gifts. Even worse, what if she fell for some Neanderthal who wanted to hold her back?

It would be sinful for Bella to hide her light under a bushel. Anyone as multi-dimensional as Finley's sister deserved a partner who would encourage her to follow her potential and interests wherever they led her.

She cocked her head and stared at him. "I don't know what to say about your last comment. Is that what bothers you? You're afraid the notoriety from the magazine article will have women pursuing you for all the wrong reasons?"

"That's already happening. I told you about London, remember?"

"Ah. Yes." She nodded slowly. "Well, trust me. It might be aggravating to have women hurling themselves at you, but with or without the fame, a guy like you can't really fly under the radar."

"A guy like me?"

Her eyes narrowed. "Don't make me say it. You're man candy."

He bristled. "I most certainly am not." The idea was ludicrous. He wasn't physically repulsive, but he had never been the bloke who went to bed with a different woman every day of the week.

"It's not an insult," she said mildly.

"I think you meant it to be," he said slowly. "You were trying to get a rise out of me. The same as if I called you arm candy."

"That would be dumb."

"So what we have here is two reasonably pleasant-looking human beings who have thus far in their lives never been the kind to attract interest from the opposite sex. Is that it?"

"I haven't had men mailing their underwear to me," she pointed out triumphantly, as if this were some kind of backward competition.

He felt his ears turn red. "I told you. It's the damn article. The writer made me sound like a cross between a playboy billionaire and Bill Gates."

"Bill Gates isn't sexy."

"I know that!" He pounded his fist on the table. "It makes no sense." All the frustrations of the past three weeks bubbled up inside him. The loss of privacy. The inevitable ribbing from his colleagues. The feeling that something had been taken from him.

The madder he got, the more his self-control winnowed away. He was confused and horny and miles outside his comfort zone. After his outburst, Bella subsided into silence, her eyes round with astonishment.

At last, she relaxed and leaned forward to pat his hand. "It's going to be okay," she said softly. "Soon, some *real* celebrity will have an affair with a space alien. Or maybe a big-time athlete will be caught rigging a sporting event. If you're really lucky, Prince Harry might get engaged. Then all your worries will be over. You'll be yesterday's news, and life can get back to normal."

She gazed at him with a mixture of compassion and impish mischief. If he were extremely analytical, he would have to admit that she wasn't beautiful according to the traditional rubric most men used as a scale. She was neither blond nor willowy. Her breasts were average. Her nose was a trifle too strong for her small face. And her teeth were the tiniest bit crooked, as if her difficult father had never been willing to shell out for braces, or maybe the orthodontist was a quack.

"Are you interested in having sex with me?" The words tumbled from his mouth unbidden, born of some deep, aching need in his gut.

Bella didn't respond at all for at least thirty seconds. Her pupils dilated, her breathing escalated, and she paled. He saw her throat work as she swallowed. "It's not that bad, Ian. Honest. Why don't you run up to your room and invent something? That will cheer you right up. Maybe an app that helps people survive in the wilderness. Something like that…"

"I wasn't kidding," he said gruffly. "I don't want to be with you so I can *cheer up*."

"Are you saying I'm boring?"

He ground his teeth and counted to ten. "You're exasperating and argumentative and frustrating as hell. But..."

"But?"

This was it. He and Bella had reached a point of no return. Either they acted on the inconvenient, stomach-clenching desire that pulsed between them, or he had to leave. "I've always known I'm not the kind of guy who will likely get married. I would never be able to remember to take out the trash. When I'm working, I forget to eat most days. Children are a mystery to me. My father was remote and cold. I would never want to cause emotional harm to a baby because I happened to be too wrapped up in a project to be *present*."

Bella blinked. "I think I missed something. Do I strike you as the kind of woman who needs a man to take out the trash?"

He groaned. "I'm trying to be clear about my motives. I don't want to hurt you."

Her chin went up and her blue eyes glowed with heat. "What if *I* hurt *you*?"

He shouldn't have laughed. It made her mad, and that wasn't his intent at all. "I'd assumed that was a given. Judging by how much I want to see you naked right now, I'd probably walk through burning coals to have one last chance in your bed before I leave."

"You are assuming an awful lot," she said, the words icy with disdain. Still, in some little corner of his brain that wasn't thinking about sex, he recognized the flicker of uncertainty in her eyes.

"Wrong," he said flatly. "I'm asking. Maybe another man would *take* first and ask questions later. I don't know. But you're Finley's sister, and I don't want this to get weird."

"I'll have to think about it."

The disappointment that gripped him was unprecedented. "So not tonight?"

"Not tonight," she said firmly. "We could try kissing, though. If it doesn't go well, we wouldn't have to fool with the rest."

"The rest?" Did she really mean to dismiss sex so cavalierly? Her nonchalant assumption that intimacy between them might be ho-hum set his teeth on edge...and awoke his fighting instincts. "I agree," he said sharply. "Let's get started."

She huffed, a little startled sound. Her gaze darted wildly around the kitchen. "My ankle might be broken. I don't think that's wise."

"You've been flitting around the island all afternoon. Don't be absurd. Besides, I promise not to kiss your ankle...at least not yet."

It was amazingly gratifying to see gutsy little Bella twist in the wind. His suggestive comment turned her face red as the tomato on the kitchen windowsill. She sputtered and grabbed for her crutch.

Casually, he moved it out of her reach. "You won't be needing that, my dear." He stood up from the table and watched her watch him. It was almost impossible not to smile. She was both intrigued and terrified. He could see it in her eyes and on her face.

His libido took a momentary backseat to tenderness. Scooping her into his arms, he carried her through to the living room where Finley's large comfy sofa awaited them. "Don't be afraid, lass. I'll not do anything you don't want me to do, I swear."

When he sat down with her in his lap, he was exceedingly careful not to bump her poor bruised foot. Tonight was about pleasure, not pain.

Bella plucked at a loose thread on his shirt pocket. "I'm not very good at...this," she whispered. "It's messy and unpredictable, and I never know how to let go and enjoy myself."

Her candor took him aback. "Only kissing," he said. "Remember? No need for nerves."

"You won't make fun of me? Or tease me?"

He realized she was serious. Pulling back, he scowled at her. "My God. What kind of men have you been with? I might tease you in certain situations, but it won't because you're not good at kissing or sex. You're amazing, Bella. How can you not know that?"

"You're yelling again," she said timidly, though her smile was smug. By now she had discovered the extent of his arousal. It was hard to miss with her hip pressed up against him.

He'd had it with talking. Some things were better communicated tacitly. Carefully, he unbuttoned her top. Her baby-blue bra was trimmed with black lace. He traced the top edge with a single finger, his chest heaving. This was a bad idea. A very bad idea. Somewhere between the kitchen and here, he had lost control. He wanted to lay her back on the long sofa and move on top of her.

When he slipped one bra strap down her shoulder, her eyelids fluttered and closed.

"No," he said hoarsely. "Don't go away. Stay with me." He bent his head and eased her down against the arm of the sofa so he could reach her lips. When he covered her mouth with his, she whispered his name. The sound went straight to his gut, hardening his erection a millimeter more.

Knowing that sex was off the table for tonight lent a sort of youthful unabashed experimentation to the moment. Her lips were pressed firmly together. He teased the seam with his tongue until she opened and let him in. The taste of her was intoxicating.

He had forgotten to dim the lights. Cinnamon whined from the study where he had closed her up while they ate dinner. Though Finley's cottage was nice, it was hardly a luxury suite at the Ritz. Yet somehow, the room narrowed to a quiet, erotic bubble of intimacy that held only the two of them.

Bella curled her arms around his neck. "You're nice when you're not bossing me around," she murmured, nipping his bottom lip with sharp teeth.

Shuddering, he dragged her closer. "I hope that means we've passed the kissing test." He slipped a fingertip beneath her bra and caressed one taut nipple. *Danger. Danger.* The sound blared in his head rudely.

She had told him no. He intended to respect her boundaries. One more kiss. That was all…

* * *

Bella floated on a cloud of euphoria. Her whole adult life this kind of moment had eluded her. Yet here was Ian, the contrary Scotsman, turning her world upside down.

His mouth was firm but tender. His hands learned the contours of her body. She and Ian were both mostly clothed. He'd made no move to unfasten her bra. Suddenly, she wanted to be naked, desperately wonderfully naked.

"You're a world-class kisser," she muttered. "Top marks."

"Shut up, Bella," he said pleasantly. "Shut up and kiss me."

They slid into a dream. One where nothing mattered except the beating of her heart and the harsh cadence of his breathing. She knew he was aroused. She had touched him hesitantly until he moved her hand away. It was the right thing to do. They weren't having sex tonight.

Hazily, she pondered her options. A brief, wonderful affair with Ian might be the best thing that ever happened to her. And if it went badly, they lived on different continents, so she wouldn't be subjected to the humiliation of running into him at the market or at a social gathering.

What she was feeling in this moment was new and disturbing. How could she be so aroused by a man who drove her insane on a daily basis?

She was hot and kerfuffled and about to climb out of her own skin. Recklessly, she dragged his head toward hers and kissed him wildly. His response was immediate and thrilling.

Big arms held her tightly against a body that was tautly muscled and damp with perspiration. He seemed desperate. That raw need seduced her as surely as any sweet words.

"I changed my mind," she panted. "Let's do this."

Ian froze, his big body shaking. "Don't say that, damn it. You have to be sure." He released her abruptly and stood, leaving her like a rag doll, her limbs sprawled everywhere.

Raising up on her elbows, she glared at him. "Haven't you ever heard of getting lost in the moment?" That he could be logical and mature when she was practically sobbing with the need for him made her angry and hurt. Clearly, she was far too involved.

She lurched to her feet, intending to button her shirt as she fled. But in her haste, she forgot about her ankle. When she put weight on it, she gasped in pain and lost her balance, falling against the man from whom she was trying to escape. Tears she couldn't hold back dribbled down her cheeks, completing her humiliation. "Damn you, Ian. Let me go."

He didn't state the obvious. The only thing keeping her upright at the moment was his comforting embrace. She sniffled against his shirt, feeling the sting of unappeased hunger. Lust. That's all it was. Pheromones. It was a small house. They were both young and healthy. This was bound to happen.

Gradually, she calmed. Ian stroked her hair steadily, his fingers brushing her nape. "I care about you, Bella. I don't want to be one of your regrets."

Should she believe him? Why else would he have stopped? His body gave him away. He wanted her. A man couldn't fake that kind of thing.

She swallowed her tears and her frustration. "You're right, of course. I would appreciate it if you would get me my crutch so I can go upstairs."

Still he played with her hair. "It's early yet. Why don't we sit on the front steps and look for stars?"

The leaves on the trees would make that difficult, but she was in a mood to be persuaded. "Okay, but I still want my crutch."

She sensed that her insistence bothered him. Surely he didn't expect her to lean on him forever.

"Fine," he muttered. He eased her gently into a chair. "I'll be back."

When he returned, Cinnamon trotted at his heels, her canine expression hopeful. Bella had to smile. "You're a sweet baby." The furry companion would come in handy. With the dog between them, maybe Bella wouldn't do something stupid.

The night was still and hushed. Though it was awkward, Bella used her crutch and sat down hard on the top step. Cinnamon curled up at her hip. Ian staked out a position in the other side of the dog, standing and leaning against the railing. "I miss this when I'm in the city," he said.

"Miss what?"

"The outdoors."

"You don't go outside in London? I've been there. They have parks and such."

"Of course," he said. "But Skye and the Highlands are different. Glasgow in Gaelic means dear green place."

"I didn't know that." Good grief. At this point, they would soon be discussing the weather.

"Ian?"

"Hmm?" He sounded distracted as though his thoughts were a million miles away.

"I shared with you about my novel. Will you tell me the real reason you're so keen to avoid the paparazzi?"

She saw his shoulders rise and fall and heard his deep sigh. "I suppose I must. It's no' a big secret, really."

She stayed quiet. His Scottish accent had thickened, indicating a change in his mood, though she wasn't sure why.

"I had trouble with school," he said simply. "My aptitude for numbers and reasoning developed early. Many of my teachers quite honestly didn't know what to do with me. Most of them did their best. They let me muddle along on my own…gave me advanced textbooks, that sort of thing."

"I'm guessing it's not every day a genius comes along."

"Not a genius," he protested. "But different than most."

"Okay, not a genius. Call it what you will, I'd say you ended up at one point knowing more than the instructor."

"Aye. When I was fourteen. The man thought I was smarting off to him, but honest to God, all I wanted to do was learn. One day before school he wrote out an involved equation on the board. Most of my classmates were outside, lingering to the very last instant because they hated the classes and the homework. Me, I loved it. I always went in early to get my notes in order and to be ready for the lecture. I sat down at my desk as usual, but that's when things went south."

"Tell me," she said, her heart in her throat. The image of Ian as a vulnerable young lad haunted her.

"I sat there reading the figures he had written, and I saw a mistake."

"Oh, Ian."

"It was plain as day. I didn't want him to be embarrassed when the other lads came in, so I jumped up, erased a few letters and numbers, and corrected the math. Mr. Bingham showed up as I was doing it. He was apoplectic... started screaming and calling me names. The others came running, of course. I was stupid and naïve when it came to the nuances of male pride. I had diminished him in his own classroom, and he made me pay."

"What did he do to you?"

Ian's rough laugh held little humor. "I may have forgotten to mention that I stuttered. School was often hell for me when I was forced to give an oral report or simply to answer a question verbally. You know how children can be. Not only were my abilities an affront to them, but my speech impediment gave them plenty of fodder to torment me."

Bella winced. She knew she didn't want to hear what came next, but since she had asked the question, it was too late. "Go on," she said. "Tell me."

Chapter Nine

Ian was afraid to sit down beside Bella, even with the dog between them. His blood still pumped. Sexual hunger was a living, breathing beast that rode him hard. Reliving his past was like peeling away a layer of skin. He felt raw and wretched. Still, if hearing the details of his painful adolescence helped Bella know and trust him, the catharsis might be worth it.

"Once the teacher calmed down, things became worse," he said. "We all took our seats, but I was summoned to the front of the room and forced to sit on a stool facing my classmates. You can't imagine what it was like to see their faces. Males at that age have a pack mentality. They can be led astray in the direction of evil, or inspired for good. On that particular day, the dark side won."

"You don't have to tell me the rest," Bella whispered. "Really, you don't."

He shrugged. While it was true that he was now extremely successful and respected for his work and his contributions, nothing would ever erase the memory of that long ago day or the weeks that followed. Surviving the psychological torment had required a special kind of courage. Though he had contemplated running away from home, the downside of having an advanced IQ was being able to calculate the odds of such a venture succeeding. In the end, he'd had no choice but to stay.

"Ian?"

Disappearing into the past so deeply made it a shock to hear her voice. "Sorry." Pulling himself together, he sat down on the top step and rested his elbows on his knees, scrubbing his hands over his face. "He made me explain the equation on the board in minute detail…as if I were the teacher. It was pure agony. My throat closed up. I stuttered so badly no one could understand what I was saying. The entire roomful of boys burst into laughter that went on and on and on…"

Bella uttered a curse that surprised him. "That was child abuse, Ian. The man should have been shot. I can't even imagine…"

"For the remainder of the term, he forced me to sit on the stool at the front. Every day when he put equations on the board, he made a big pretense of having me 'check' them. The unfortunate thing was, I continued to find errors. I didn't know what else to do but to correct them, which made him more and more determined to teach me a lesson."

"We'd call that bullying now. No one would stand for it."

Ian shook his head at her naiveté. "There is good and bad in all of us, you know. It's shockingly easy to turn a crowd into a mob. Boys I considered my friends turned away from me, because I had become a pariah. They couldn't afford to be seen with me, for fear they would end up on the wrong side of an imaginary line."

"How did you bear it?"

He shrugged. "The ostracism helped me in one way…made me more determined to score the highest marks…to learn far beyond what was required of me"

"I am so sorry."

"I don't need anyone's pity," he said sharply. "As an adult, I paid for speech therapy that eliminated almost every vestige of my disability. The stutter only resurfaces in very stressful situations."

She gasped audibly. "That's why you're so determined to elude the reporters," she said. "You don't want to stutter on camera."

"In a nutshell, yes. It's bad enough they can splash my photograph over every media outlet, social and otherwise. I cringe at the headlines that *could* be written. *Eligible Bachelor number two c-c-an n-n-ot t-t-talk to women.*"

Before Bella could respond to his dark humor, the sound of a vehicle climbing the hill broke the silence. Finley's was the only house here at the top. He owned several acres that served as a buffer for his privacy. Nevertheless, the car continued upward.

As it came into view, Bella got to her feet clumsily and used her crutch to hobble down the steps. When the car door opened, a woman jumped out and flung herself at Bella, nearly knocking her down. The surprise visitor cried out in an anguished voice. "It's wee Jackie, Bella. He's disappeared. I dinna know what to do." Ian recognized Hilda, Bella's friend who had dropped by earlier that day.

They got her inside, and Ian fetched a cup of tea. Bella held the red-haired woman's hands and chafed them. "Tell us what happened."

Hilda's hands shook so badly the cup clattered in the saucer, but she drank the tea anyway. "My mother-in-law brought the boys back just before dinner. They'd had a lovely day. The boys were knackered, but they gobbled down their meal, so that put a bit of life back into them. Jackie Sr. and I were dabblin' about in the kitchen. The boys were in front of the telly for a half hour show. I went to check on them and Jackie was gone."

Ian inserted himself into the conversation. "I assume you've called the police."

Hilda nodded. "They're organizing volunteer search parties to comb the town. My big Jack is with them. Me mother-in-law has the wee one. I thought Bella might wander this hill with me. Ye know how the child likes to climb. But I forgot about your foot."

Ian touched her shoulder briefly. "Of course we'll help. Bella will need to stay here, but I can cover a large area on my own."

Hilda sobbed quietly now, her eyes closed, her head lolling against the back of the sofa. Ian suspected she was in shock.

Bella stood and motioned for Ian to follow her to the far corner of the room. "I'm not staying here," she hissed, her eyes flashing blue sparks at him. "I know the area far better than you do."

He tamped down his temper. In an emergency situation, calm had to prevail. "How old is the child?"

"Four. Almost five. He's been a handful from the time he was born according to the stories I've heard. Climbed out of his crib before he was a year old. Learned how to unlatch the doors at two. Slipped away from his mum on market day last year and ended up on a fisherman's boat that was anchored in the harbor. He could be anywhere."

Ian frowned. "Is kidnapping a possibility?"

"Not likely. Besides, most of the town knows Jackie. If anyone noticed him wandering around, they would have called Hilda."

"But he's been gone for two, maybe three hours by now?"

"Yes, I suppose."

Ian felt adrenaline kick in. He knew what it was like to feel lost and alone, even if his situation had been more mental than physical. "Send your friend back to her house. Tell her she needs to be there in case the boy returns unannounced. I'll grab some gear upstairs and be on my way."

When he came back down five minutes later, Bella stood by the front door, crutch-free, her face pale and her chin outthrust. She had managed to put on tennis shoes, despite her injured foot. Before he could say anything, she held out her hand. "You can't make me stay here. I'm going. So get used to the idea. The foot's not broken. It's only a sprain. I'm fine."

Ian grimaced, torn between the need to protect her and the knowledge that she was right. He *did* need someone who knew the area. "If you end up slowing me down, I won't be able to carry you. A child spending the night outdoors on an early autumn night like this runs the risk of hypothermia. Every minute will count."

"I understand."

Hell, who was he kidding. If he had to, he would search for the boy with Bella on his back. She didn't need to know that, though.

They exited the house without further argument. Bella walked gingerly, but with increasing confidence. She must have taken a pain pill. Otherwise she would never have been able to tolerate abusing her injury.

The hilltop was heavily wooded. Cinnamon liked to roam around up there. They brought her along, although the large dog had no formal search and rescue training. Nevertheless, her canine hearing and smell could prove to be helpful if they could keep her youthful exuberance under control.

Because of the nature of their search, they moved around Finley's house in ever-widening circles, careful not to miss a single square meter. After an hour and a half, they had seen no sign that *anyone* had been in the area recently.

Winded and sweaty, they sat down together against two trees and reconnoitered. Ian had slung a small backpack over his shoulder. He offered a bottle of water to Bella and opened one for himself.

She was quieter than usual. He knew she was worried. "*Someone* will find him," he said. "He couldn't have gone far."

"It's not a friendly place in the dark," she fretted. "Cliffs and water are a terrible combination for a kid with no fear." She took a long swig of water and wiped her mouth. "What's that thing you've been using?"

He finished his water, capped the bottle, and stowed it in his pack to be recycled. "It's a prototype I'm working on. It uses infrared technology to pick up heat signatures. The military already utilizes a form of this, but my design integrates GPS and algorithms that filter out distractions like squirrels and other animals. It's keeping track of every inch we've searched and will be able to tell me if we missed anything."

"Impressive."

"It's only good if it works. Come on. Unless you need to stay here?"

He made it a question. No harm would come to her.

Bella sprang to her feet with little grace but lots of determination. "I'm right behind you."

* * *

Bella's heart sank with each passing minute. Her cell phone remained silent in her pocket. She had explained to Hilda exactly what she and Ian planned to do. Hilda would have called if Jackie had been found.

They were running out of places to look. On the backside of Finley's hill, the land sloped sharply toward the water. They were forced to cling to trees in order to make their way downward. It was slow, tedious progress.

"Stop here," Ian insisted. "The dirt is loose. If you fall again, you could seriously damage your foot." He looked at the dog. "Stay with her Cinnamon. Understand?"

The dog whined, indicating agreement. Either that or a request for a doggie treat.

Bella knew that what Ian said made sense, though she didn't like it. She dared not look at her ankle. She could tell it was swollen like a small blimp. Her bottom lip throbbed where she had bitten it repeatedly, a nervous habit. It was impossible to imagine what Hilda and her husband were going through.

Though it was dark, Bella could see Ian's shadowy figure descending carefully. Without warning he stopped and called out to her. "I need your help. Get down here. But easy. Hold on to everything you can."

She and Cinnamon hurried to obey the urgency in Ian's voice. When they finally made it to his side, he was crouched, using his prototype to scan the area below. "What is it?" she whispered. There was no particular need for discretion, but her stomach was in a knot.

"I see something about twenty feet below us. It looks like a clump of bushes growing out over the water. I'm picking up a heat signal that's fairly large. It could be him."

"But if he's asleep or unconscious, we can't startle him."

"Exactly. If he moves, he could fall. I can't tell how much farther it is to the water, and I don't know if he can swim."

Bella gripped Cinnamon's leash until her fingers were numb. "What are we going to do?"

Ian's reply was terse and determined. "I'll rappel down and get him. No worries."

The next five minutes were a blur. Ian had remembered seeing nylon rope in Finley's workshop and had brought it along. With Bella's assistance, he tied himself into a makeshift harness, secured the rope around a good-sized tree, and tested the knots.

She took his shoulders and kissed him lightly. "Feel free to be a hero, but don't do anything stupid. It might not even be him."

Ian broke free of her hold as if he couldn't afford to be distracted. "Of course it's him. Who else could it be?"

"A very large skunk?"

"Let's hope not."

Ian's descent took far longer than Bella anticipated. He had to move with agonizing care to avoid kicking loose debris down onto his target. Consequently, it was more like twenty minutes than ten before he reached his destination.

It was so dark she could see virtually nothing. Knowing that unknown water lurked underneath the rescue attempt made the whole thing worse. Her eyes ached from trying to peer below. At last the prearranged signal came. Ian had told her to expect two firm tugs on the rope when he was ready to ascend.

Even she and Cinnamon working together were little help. Ian was pulling himself, unaided, up the steep hillside, carrying something... someone. Please God, let it be Jackie, and let him be okay.

Ian might be a hermit-nerd, as Finley had coined the term, but he was also a man's man, physically strong and ready to face a grueling challenge at a moment's notice. She prayed incoherently, especially when Ian and his burden were almost to the top and Ian's foot slipped.

"Are you okay?" she cried out.

"I'm fine," he said, his voice strained and winded. "I think the poor bairn has a broken arm."

At last, the two males made it onto solid ground. Ian laid the boy in Bella's arms. He had taken off his coat and wrapped it around the child, but Jackie whimpered softly as though he were cold or in pain or both. Cinnamon licked the boy's face. The dog then sidled up to Bella's hip and stood guard.

Ian untied himself and stuffed all the gear haphazardly into the backpack. "Do you have a phone signal?" he asked.

"No. Already checked. We'll have to get to the top of the hill for a clear shot."

"Damn it. His parents are going through hell."

She put a hand on his arm where the muscles were tense. "We're doing the best we can. Thanks to you, he's going to okay."

"We don't know that yet. I'm not a doctor. Let's get going."

Their progress uphill was excruciatingly slow. Ian moved from tree to tree, cradling Jackie in his left arm and steadying himself with his right hand. The strength and energy it must be taking to accomplish such a feat astonished Bella. Ian didn't mention her foot again, and she was glad. Her injury paled under the circumstances. Yes, she was in pain. And yes, it was possible she had significantly delayed her recovery. But she would do it all again.

Cinnamon was a huge help. Bella clutched the end of the leash in her free hand and let the dog pull her up. For the young animal who was barely older than a puppy, the whole nighttime excursion probably seemed like a lark. Truthfully, though, Cinnamon's usual exuberance was muted as though she recognized the gravity of the situation.

At the top of the hill they paused for Bella to contact Hilda. The call signal still wasn't strong, so she sent a text instead:

Come quickly. My house. We have Jackie.

Then they set out across the last hundred yards. They had no more than made it to Finley's front porch when a cavalcade of vehicles appeared in the drive. With no real parking available, cars were abandoned wherever they stopped. Hilda and her husband led the charge. They jumped out and ran.

Jackie's father extended his arms. "Let me have him. Is he...?"

Gently, Ian handed over the boy. "I think he has a broken arm. He's semiconscious, but his pulse is strong. Is there a doctor nearby?"

An older woman stepped forward. "I'm the doctor. I'd like to take him inside for the exam if I may."

"Of course," Bella said. "The door's open."

Jackie's parents, the tiny patient, and the doctor went inside.

For a moment, the crowd of townspeople was silent. Then pandemonium broke out. "Tell us where you found him," someone yelled.

"Where was the boy?"

"Did he say anything?"

The questions went on and on. Bella tried to answer as many as she could. Ian was at her side, but slightly behind her. He didn't say a word. Though the hour was late, several cars had left their headlights on, illuminating the unfolding rescue scene. Both traditional cameras and smartphones flashed. Everyone wanted a record of the day's events.

Suddenly, three men pushed forward from the fringes of the group. Bella recognized them instantly. They were the same annoying reporters who had showed up on her doorstep and later tried to ambush Ian at the restaurant.

Bella's spine stiffened in outrage. This time there was no escape route.

The most aggressive of the trio shoved his way through the crowd and stopped right in front of her. "I want the name of the bloke who rescued the kid. It's Larrimore, isn't it? Ian Larrimore?"

Still, Ian said nothing. Bella frowned. "He would prefer to remain anonymous."

The man shot a glance at Ian. For a moment, the reporter wavered as if abashed by his own persistence. Then he literally shouldered Bella aside and shoved a microphone in Ian's face. "Tell us what it feels like to be one of Britain's most eligible bachelors and a hero on top of that. Your adoring public wants to know."

Short of turning his back and walking away, Ian had no choice but to respond. Bella's fists clenched at her sides. She was fiercely protective of her houseguest and violently angry at the scurrilous quasi-newsman.

Ian's body language was an amalgam of outrage, icy disdain, and utter distaste. But in the dark, and with the artificial glare of the headlights, Bella was likely the only one who read him correctly. He cleared his throat. "I'm not a h-h-hero. I'm just deeply glad the l-l-l-ad is safe."

To the listening crowd, it seemed as if Ian was overcome with emotion. Only Bella knew the truth. She held up her hands. "Please give Hilda and Jack some space. It's been a very difficult few hours. Thank you for your concern."

The onlookers muttered and began dispersing. Bella turned around to speak to Ian, but he was gone.

Chapter Ten

Ian stumbled into the house and wiped his face with his hands. His body ached. He had scrapes and scratches. Worst of all, he was embarrassed. He'd left Bella to handle the mess outside. What kind of man did that?

Hilda jumped up from the sofa. Her small son lay with his head resting in his father's lap. The man stroked the child's forehead. The doctor talked to the boy in a soft voice. Hilda flung her arms around Ian and hugged him until his ribs threatened to crack. "Thank you, thank you, Mr. Larrimore. My son nearly died. I'm forever in yer debt."

"How did you know my name?"

The ghost of a grin painted Hilda's face despite her emotional trauma. "Bella refused to confirm yer presence, but Portree's a small town. Word gets around. I don't know how we'll ever repay you for savin' our boy."

"Anybody could have found him," Ian said, shifting from one foot to the other. "I'm honored I could help."

She squeezed hard and released him at last, allowing him to breathe. "I know ye must be jiggered after what ye did. Took a lot of brute strength. Go on now and get some rest."

Ian knew he should wait for Bella, but he was raw and wavering on the edge of an explosion. He'd come to Finley's house in the back of beyond to hide out. Now, not only was his cover blown, but he'd unwittingly become embroiled in a town drama.

He loped up the stairs to his room and stared blankly at the space that had seemed a refuge. Or maybe it was a prison. He wasn't sure. All he knew was that he wanted to get away from here.

It was the same feeling he'd had in London, only worse. Bella must think him the most awkward fool. A grown man who couldn't answer a simple question on camera without stammering.

Pacing the confines of the small room, he was completely unable to calm himself. His agitation grew worse and worse until at last, he cursed and punched the wall as hard as he could.

The outburst produced a variety of outcomes. Tiny flecks of dust littered the floor, but the plaster got the best end of the deal. Ian's knuckles split and bled. Pain shot up his arm and lingered to throb along every nerve from his fingers to his shoulder.

His humiliation was complete when he turned and found Bella standing in the open doorway, eyes round, expression aghast. "Ian," she cried. "What did you do to yourself?"

He put his hand behind his back, feeling slightly ill. "Nothing. Will you go now, please?"

She ignored his belligerence and came to him, taking his injured hand in both of hers and examining it carefully. "Oh, Ian. What a mess you've made." Her concern and gentle care should have made him feel better. Instead, he wanted to howl his frustration.

Bella was right. It was true. Not only had he showed rank cowardice in fleeing London, he had done something even worse. He had let a curvy, opinionated woman with big blue eyes and masses of raven-wing hair worm her way into his heart.

And to what end?

"Leave me alone," he muttered. "I'm fine."

"I'm so sorry, Ian."

Her sympathy felt like alcohol poured on a raw wound. She wasn't talking about his bloodied hand. Bella had witnessed him revert to a stuttering school boy when pinned down by the dogged little reporter.

He shrugged, not meeting her eyes. He didn't want her kindness or her understanding. Harsh-toned words blurted from his lips unfiltered. "I'm going home," he said. "Tonight. I'll drive to Inverness and catch the early train in the morning."

Bella froze. Her face paled, and her eyes sheened with tears. "Why, Ian? What's the point? They got what they came for. They'll leave you alone now. Don't go…please."

He put his hands on her shoulders and set her aside, trying not to notice how small and fragile she felt. "I have work to do."

"What about us?"

Her question stopped him dead in his tracks. His jaw worked. "There isn't really any *us*," he said flatly. "We flirted with the concept, but we never made it to the prototype. I've interfered with your time in Scotland. Let's reset the clock. It's the wisest thing to do."

Bella practically went up in smoke. She glared at him. "Heaven forbid that the mighty Ian Larrimore should ever do anything unwise. You're a horse's ass. You stuttered a bit. So what? I was the only one who realized. Everyone else thought you were feeling torn up about what happened."

"You don't understand." He pulled his suitcase out from under the bed and began tossing things in haphazardly.

Bella thumped his back with her fist. "I understand more than you think. You've spent your whole life believing you're a superior intellect. Turns out, you're just as clueless as the next guy. It's okay not to be perfect. I like you the way you are."

He whirled to face her, tormented. "I don't give a damn if you *like* me," he shouted.

She gaped at him, her beautiful, soft pink lips forming a perfect O. A single tear rolled down her cheek, driving the final nail in his coffin. "Okay, then," she whispered, her gaze tragic. "I'd rather have the whole house to myself anyway," she said. "Good-bye, Ian."

It was the limp that got to him. That and the brave set of her shoulders. Bella Craig was so damn spunky and so utterly unable to protect herself from emotional harm. What other woman of his acquaintance would be so open about her feelings? What other woman would let him know so candidly that she cared?

Watching her walk toward the door seemed to last forever. Everything inside him turned to ash. He was terrible at relationships. If he stayed, he would mess things up. He knew it. The sensible thing to do would be to leave her alone...let some other man snatch her up and make her his.

The thought of that literally set his teeth on edge. Bella was his. There was no rhyme or reason to the feeling, but he recognized its gut-deep validity.

"Wait," he croaked. "Stop."

Bella hesitated and turned around. He felt deep shame when he saw the way she regarded him. He'd been rude and cruel. She braced visibly for another volley. "What?" she asked quietly. "What else is there to say?"

He lifted his shoulders and let them fall, his hands jammed in his pockets. "I want you."

"Is that supposed to make me feel special?"

His neck grew hot. "I've wanted other women," he said slowly. "But until I came here and met you, I've never considered the possibility of a relationship. I never wanted to risk it. I'm barely thirty-five, but I'm set in my ways. I'm not easy to get along with. The female brain is a mystery to me."

"No one ever mentioned a relationship," she said. Every nuance of expression had been wiped from her face. He couldn't read her at all. "You and I considered the possibility of a fling, but that's off the table now."

"Why?" he asked urgently. "Why is it off the table?"

She lifted her chin. "Because you're a pompous ass and a lily-livered coward."

"You sound like an American Southern belle when you say that. Though it's true," he said hastily. "I'm no bargain." He ran his hands through his hair, feeling as if he were being torn apart and reassembled in the image of a man he didn't know. "Give me another chance," he said softly.

"Long distance relationships never work. You in London. Me here. It's pointless."

Was she deliberately misunderstanding him? He picked up the suitcase and dumped the contents on the bed. "I'll stay."

"Don't expect me to dance a jig over *that* news." Her nose wrinkled as if she smelled an unpleasant odor.

"I had a few bad moments. I'm feeling better now."

"You were angry that I saw you at your worst," she said. "You pitched a tantrum because of injured male pride."

He swallowed hard. "Give a guy a break."

"I've had enough drama in my short life, Ian. Most of it from men who professed to care about me. So forgive me if I don't rush to accept your apology. Although now that I think about it, you never *actually* said you were sorry for anything, did you?"

"Lord, you're pretty when you get all worked up."

"And don't patronize me," she yelled. "If you think you can blink at me with those long eyelashes and expect me to sleep with you, you're insane."

"We wouldn't do much sleeping," he vowed, closing the distance between them. "Not with you in my bed or vice versa."

When her mouth did that cute little O thing again, he kissed her gently. "I am so very sorry for being a beast to you tonight. I don't want to go to London, Bella. Not at all."

He kept his hands on her upper arms. His emotional state was wobbly, and he didn't want to do something they would both regret.

She bit her bottom lip. "You came here to hide out," she said. "If that's no longer feasible, why would you stay?"

"You know why." He folded her close, pulling her against his chest and sighing deeply. "Let's start over. Can we? Me not a fugitive. You not a reluctant innkeeper. Can't we just be a man and a woman who happened to meet on the Isle of Skye and decide to explore a connection?"

She was quiet for a very long time, but her arms remained linked around his waist and her cheek rested over his heart. "Would that make it a Highland fling?"

He groaned. "Puns. Really?" His mood lightened. "Fling. Rendezvous. Any word you want to use."

"If we start over, that means no sex for the immediate future."

He nodded glumly. "I know. You don't do that on a first date."

"Or a second or a third."

"You drive a hard bargain, woman."

"I don't take sex casually."

"You don't take *anything* casually," he pointed out. "But I like that about you," he said hastily.

She pulled back and smiled up at him, her gaze misty. "Nice save, Bachelor number two. I'll bet it drives you nuts not to be number one... your competitive nature and all that. I suppose you could try to bump Prince Harry out of the top spot, but it wouldn't be easy."

"You're making fun of me."

"Maybe a little." Her grin was cheeky.

He ran his thumb over her bottom lip, realizing he had stepped away from what might have been the most monumental mistake of his life. "I really am sorry, Bella. My only excuse is that tonight was intense. I wasn't at all sure we were going to be able to get to little Jackie. I worried about his arm. Then all hell broke loose with the cameras and the people. It was like a very bad dream."

"I understand. I think. But next time you're about to flip out, how about giving me some warning?"

"I promise."

"Okay, then," she said. "Welcome to Portree. My name is Bella Craig. I'm Finley's sister."

* * *

Bella was trying to lighten the mood, but something in Ian's eyes told her he wasn't so easily tamed. His apology had been sincere. She had no doubt of that. Still, he was honest about what he wanted from her. Sex. Plain and simple. Between them, his arousal pulsed, hard and ready.

If she kissed him, would he see it as invitation?

Fortunately, he took the decision out of her hands. "Come here, lovely Bella," he said. "I need to taste you again. I've got a hankering for your unique blend of tart and sweet."

Somewhere along the line, she got lost in what she was supposed to say or do. Reason and logic disappeared beneath a wave of yearning that honestly terrified her. She didn't want to get involved with a man who was so complicated. Did she really have a choice?

Her body said no.

Ian took his time with her…as if they had never quarreled…as if this really were simple and sweet. He held her head in two hands, tilting her face to his, using his long talented fingers to trace the whorls of her ears.

Though his touch was almost chaste, somehow he managed to light a wildfire that consumed them. Her arms twined around his neck. Her breasts ached to be touched. Her clothes were too hot.

Kissing was supposed to be romantic and fun. Not this. Ian was intent on destroying her resistance. Even knowing that, she didn't want him to stop. He was everything she had looked for in a mythical mate. Like a warrior clansman, he was big and strong and physically superior. He never used his strength for harm, but instead, to protect and cherish.

Like the knights in her textbooks, he made her feel the vanquished maiden. Her femininity went to war with her feminist sensibilities. Since when did a modern woman swoon with delight?

Perhaps since the man in question kissed like a dream and made her feel as if his entire existence might be in jeopardy if she didn't give him what he wanted. He backed her toward the bed, sliding his hands underneath her shirt and finding the clasp on her bra. "Just this," he pleaded. "Just this."

When his fingers brushed her nipples, she moaned. It felt so good she wanted to cry out. Her body was on fire. Future or no future, she didn't care. Ian was hers for the here and now, and that was enough.

"Undress me," she whispered. "Please."

He rested his forehead against hers, his whole body quivering. "Not in the heat of the moment. I don't want you to throw that in my face."

"I won't. I swear. I was kidding about the three dates. I know you, Ian. Or I know enough of you. Let's not waste any more time."

She knew deep down that this was no happily-ever-after. And it was okay. Ian was a unique man who had crossed her orbit at this moment in time. She'd be a fool to let him go.

He muttered some words that sounded like Gaelic, something rough and heartfelt. She didn't want a translation. She didn't want to hear *his* doubts and misgivings. She had plenty of her own.

With a groan, he rolled off the bed and stripped down to his knit boxers with dizzying efficiency. His body was toned and beautiful, rippled with muscles, sleek with golden skin lightly dusted with hair.

She licked her lips. "I thought science nerds were pale and pasty."

His grin was feral. "I have a villa on Mykonos. Nothing fancy. Nice for a winter getaway."

"I should say so." The admission on his part reminded her why he was on that stupid list. This was no absentminded professor smelling of mothballs and muttering indecipherable formulas. Ian Larrimore was the second most eligible bachelor in all the British Isles. He was handsome, wealthy, and fascinating. Women everywhere would give anything to be in her shoes. Bella Craig had found the golden ticket.

A little voice in the back of her brain reminded her that if something sounded too good to be true it probably was. She ignored the warning. Nothing was going to stop her now.

Not even her own sense of self-preservation.

He sat down at her hip and lazily unbuttoned her top. She and Ian were both streaked with dirt and covered in scratches. She probably had leaves and twigs in her hair, because he certainly did.

"Should we clean up first?" she asked mildly, as if she weren't on fire from the inside out.

His pained wince told her he didn't give a damn if they both were less than daisy fresh. "Is that what you want?"

"Maybe later," she muttered.

"Thank God." He bent his head and kissed her breasts, not bothering to remove her skimpy bra. The fact that he suckled her through the damp fabric struck her as unbearably erotic.

She struggled with the zipper on her jeans. At least she was wearing nice undies. The random thought made her want to laugh…right up until the moment Ian lifted her like a rag doll and unfastened her bra. He held her close, the bra trapped between them. "Is something wrong?" she asked timidly when he didn't move.

"Not exactly." He sounded winded.

"Can I help?" They had been rushing toward a delicious precipice, but now the momentum slowed.

"Do you know who the Incredible Hulk is?" he asked.

The random question confused her. "More or less, though I'm not sure what he has to do with getting me out of my clothes."

He kissed her temple. "Bruce Banner was the scientist in the comic series. Whenever he was subjected to extreme emotional stress, he morphed into a huge green monster."

"I like that you're naked, Ian, but your timing sucks. Save the bedtime stories for later."

He chuckled hoarsely. "I'm trying to tell you how I feel. Since I rarely go down that road, I thought an illustration might come in handy."

She pulled back far enough to see his face. "I'm stressing you out?" She frowned. Not what a woman wanted to hear.

"There's good stress and bad stress. I'm afraid of hurting you or scaring you. It seems like you're not all that experienced."

"So?" He wasn't wrong.

"So, I don't want to go all Incredible Hulk on you. When a man wants a woman really badly, he has a hard time being gentle."

A frisson of excitement made her shiver. "You're that wound up? Honestly?"

"Oh, yeah. I could lock you in this room and make love to you all night."

"What's stopping you?"

Chapter Eleven

The impudent question flipped some kind of switch in Ian's brain. He forgot about the rescue and the reporters and his screwed up life. All he could think about was Bella. How soft she was. How she smelled like roses in springtime. The amazing way her mind worked. The wonder of nature that was her feminine, curvy body.

Her skin was cool beneath his fingertips, maybe because he was hotter than hot. Talk was getting him nowhere. If anything, he had worried her. Carefully, he tugged at the bra and tossed it on the floor.

His chest heaved. "Lift your hips, lass. Let's get rid of these pants."

The quiet happiness in her eyes said she knew a delicious secret. He'd expected her to be on the shy side in bed. If anything, he was the one who found himself in uncharted waters.

Bella was unlike any woman he had ever known. She challenged him intellectually, while at the same time driving him half mad with wanting her. When she was completely nude, he removed his boxers. Joining her in the bed, he flipped back the covers so she couldn't hide from him.

He put his hand, palm flat on her belly. "You're awfully quiet for a woman who has an opinion about everything."

"Fishing for compliments?" She taunted him with a smirk.

"Fine," he grumbled. "Don't talk. I have plans for your mouth anyway." Behind her bold façade, he could swear he saw uncertainty. The notion wounded him. What would it take to make her want this moment as much as he did? "Turn over on your stomach," he said.

She blinked once. "Okay."

Now he was treated to a canvas of curves and shadows, a masterpiece of pale skin and tousled dark hair. He straddled her legs and put his hands between her shoulder blades. "Let me know if this is too much."

Bella made some little muffled noise that could have been assent. It certainly didn't seem as if she wanted him to stop. He aligned his thumbs along either side of her spine and pressed deeply.

Her moan made him smile. At one time, early in his early academic career, he had considered medicine as a life path. Other disciplines eventually lured him away, but he still remembered most of his anatomy studies. Such a thing came in handy when a man wanted to pleasure a woman.

Touching her was both bliss and torment. The silky feel of her skin beneath his fingertips was too visceral, too real. He didn't want to have this experience burned into his brain. That was something women did... sentimentalizing sex. He was a man of intellect. His brain told him this was going to be physical and satisfying. End of story.

Bella sighed and stretched her arms above her head. "If I were any looser, I'd slide off the bed and onto the floor. High marks as a masseuse, Mr. Larrimore. If you ever need a reference, I'm happy to oblige."

"I haven't gotten to the good parts yet. Roll on your side and face me, lass. I'm even better from that angle." He moved away from her and reclined, his head propped on his hand.

She made a noise halfway between a snort and a laugh, but obeyed. Now, it was worse. Not only could he touch her endlessly, but he could look into her eyes. Had she learned some kind of mesmerist's trick? Why else did his throat dry and his hands shake when their gazes locked? What was she thinking? What did she expect from him?

The bed was comfortable, though the room was hardly decked out for seduction. The overhead fixture cast a harsh glare. Perhaps with candlelight and rose petals he could have made a better impression.

Lightly, he mapped the curves of her plump breasts. Bella caught her breath, her cheeks flushing. "You needn't keep up the foreplay, Ian. I'm ready. Completely."

"You don't like what I'm doing?" The lazy pace cost him, ratcheting up his hunger and making him clumsy. It reassured him in some odd way that Bella was no more comfortable than he was with the intimate situation. They were both lamentably awkward when it came to verbal cues. Hopefully, they would excel in the next, more hands-on phase.

She caught his wrist and squeezed it tightly. "Seriously, Ian. I want you. Now."

This time there was no joking tone in her voice, no humorous digs at his expense. Her clarity satisfied him somehow. It was gratifying not to have to guess what a woman was thinking. Bella was real and honest and beautifully direct in her explicit demand.

His sex pulsed. His heart raced. Hands trembling, he reached into the bedside table for protection. Bella averted her eyes as he took care of the matter. That little show of bashful embarrassment brought tenderness back into the mix. For all her intelligence and book smarts, she betrayed her sheltered upbringing at times.

"If I do something you don't like, you have to tell me." He tucked her hair behind her ear. "Understood?"

She nodded, big-eyed. "Yes, Ian." When she licked her lips, he nearly lost it. Staring at him like a kid about to choose an ice cream flavor, she moved her thighs apart and held out her arms. "No more talking."

It was a damned fine plan. He'd lost the ability to speak, anyway. He touched her carefully and found her damp and ready. When he fit the head of his erection to her center and pushed slowly, time slowed to a crawl.

Holy hell. Her body welcomed him, though Bella's slight wince told him she had not practiced this particular sport in recent months. He grew dizzy, weak. But at the same time, a great wave of exultation built in his chest. This woman. Finley's sister. Bossy. Brave. Impossible to predict. She made him want like he had never wanted before.

Things got hazy after that. He remembered thrusting wildly when she linked her ankles behind his back. There might have been a moment when he bit the side of her neck and panted, trying desperately to hold back the need to come that pummeled him relentlessly.

Breathless, exultant, he found his release and shouted her name.

After that, he slept.

* * *

Bella gathered her clothes and limped out of the room, pausing to lower the lights as she departed. Ian was dead to the world. His body had been a considerable but pleasant weight on top of her. The fact that she still quivered with unsatisfied needs was not really his fault. She had told him she was ready. In fact, she had insisted he get to the main event.

The poor man couldn't have known that she was so nervous she felt like puking or fainting, or both.

In retrospect, the massage had been the best part. Having Ian touch her so deliberately and sweetly lit a spark deep inside her belly that threatened to turn into a conflagration. Unfortunately, her lack of experience in the bedroom had sabotaged her.

A savvier woman would have taken his hands and put them here or there or everywhere, demanding what she wanted and needed. Unfortunately, Bella had been so caught up in the sheer craziness of having this gorgeous man claiming her with out-of-control enthusiasm that she had allowed herself to be left behind. She certainly wasn't going to wake him now and demand he finish her off with a flourish. The brave Scotsman had rescued a child from near-tragic circumstances. Ian needed his rest.

Once she made it back to the relative safety of the master suite, she bolted the door and headed for the bathroom. Fortunately, there was no one to see if she shed a tear or two underneath the stinging spray of the shower. She soaped her body and shampooed her hair, all the while trying to forget that Ian had stroked her here and touched her there.

She could count on one hand the times she had been intimate with a man... and still have two fingers left over. Clearly, she wasn't cut out for sexual liaisons. Though she had learned to stand up for herself with her domineering father and also in the world of academia, physical relationships with the opposite sex were harder to negotiate.

The unintentional pun made her laugh, even though she still felt like crying. It was a good bet Ian thought everything was fine. She certainly wasn't going to disabuse him of that notion.

Despite the adrenaline-filled hours of the day that had now passed into history, Bella had trouble sleeping. Her ankle throbbed, though she had taken a pain pill. Not only that, but she was accustomed to the muted sounds of traffic near her downtown condo back in North Carolina. The scream of sirens heading to the nearby hospital. Laughter and loud voices from the outside patio of the trendy restaurant next door.

Here on Skye, the nights were deep and quiet. She honestly hadn't realized how noisy her modern life *was*. Closing her eyes, she started counting all the sheep she had encountered on island roads thus far.

Eventually, she slept...

* * *

Things looked marginally better in the morning. If she could convince Ian that she was blasé about the whole "scratch an itch" experiment last night, maybe he wouldn't make a big deal about it.

To that end, she brewed a large pot of coffee, settled down at the kitchen table with her favorite Scottish guidebook, and waited. It was almost nine when Ian finally appeared in the doorway. He was bleary-eyed and surprisingly unkempt for Britain's #2 bachelor.

His hair stood on end. The shirt he wore was wrinkled. As far as she could tell he had crawled straight out of bed without even bothering to take a shower. Considering his role in Jackie's rescue, along with his later amorous activities, surely the man needed some soap and water.

"Good morning, Ian." She gave him a serene smile and returned her attention to the page she was reading.

"I woke up and you were gone."

The accusation held a mixture of bewilderment and pique. Clearly her houseguest slept like the proverbial log. She had returned to her own room hours and hours ago. This was the first time he noticed?

It occurred to her he had no idea she had fled after sex last night. Buoyed by his ignorance, she managed an airy wave. "Busy day. Lots to do. I made a big pot of coffee. Shall I fix you some toast?"

"Don't want any toast," he mumbled. After pouring himself a drink in the largest mug the cottage had to offer, Ian dropped down in the chair opposite Bella's. "You were gone when I woke up." He reiterated his complaint.

Bella decided to ignore him. She sipped her now-cold beverage and read the same page four times. It was one of the few occasions she and Ian had actually shared the breakfast table. They both liked silence in the mornings. Eating the initial meal in shifts had been the order of the day.

It was impossible to pretend he wasn't in the room, though she tried. It was also impossible not to think about him naked. *Sweet heaven.* For a man whose claims to fame were his IQ, his outward good looks, and his bank balance, it seemed unfair to other men that beneath the slightly scruffy clothing he wore, Ian Larrimore was built like a living, breathing god. Broad shoulders, flat belly, narrow hips, and below the waist...wow. Beneath the table, her knees pressed together instinctively.

For twenty minutes Ian drank coffee and eyed her over the rim of his cup. The effort to appear calm and relaxed taxed her limited repertoire of acting skills. She felt as she were on trial. If he hoped to break her with some childish staring contest, he had no clue how desperate she was to shake off the vestiges of last night.

Eventually, he gave up. He thumped his earthenware mug on the table and drummed his fingers on the scarred wood. His jaw squared off and his eyes blazed. "I want to know why you left, damn it."

Her brow creased. "I don't understand. I needed to take a shower. What's the big deal?"

He blinked, clearly shocked that someone other than a man would be so cavalier about a booty call. "I thought women liked to cuddle."

She gave him a sweet smile. "You're being silly, Ian. We're housemates, not roommates." Flipping open her notebook, she started jotting down ideas for day trips she wanted to make, along with the longer overnight ventures. Fortunately, her brother Finley didn't expect her to stay here every minute of every day.

Ian refilled his coffee and sat back down, cradling the mug between his hands. "I'll never understand the female mind," he said, his lips curling in a wry, self-deprecatory grin. "But for the record, I wish you had lingered this morning. I was disappointed when I woke up. I missed you."

"Sorry," she mumbled. His honest confession made her question her behavior and her motives. Was his sincerity for real?

"What are you working on?" he asked. His tone was curious now, less combative than when he first showed up in the kitchen. The caffeine must have kicked in.

"Well, my month and a half is flying by. I decided I'd better plan out my remaining itinerary at least loosely, or I'll never fit in everything I want to do before I leave. Who knows when I'll have a chance to return?"

Ian reached over and filched her piece of paper. He studied it in silence. "You left off Edinburgh," he said, frowning slightly.

"Edinburgh is a big city. I thought I'd stick to the little out-of-the-way spots. Like Portree."

He crumpled up the list and tossed it in the general direction of the trash can. "I don't want to cramp your style, Bella. I've already invaded what you thought was going to be your private time at your brother's house. But…"

He trailed off tantalizingly.

"But what?"

"I have a proposition for you," he said.

Everything inside her went on red alert. "Excuse me?"

Instead of answering, he stood up and paced. A couple of times he opened his mouth as if he were going to speak, but nothing came out.

At last, she lost patience. "What is this proposition?"

"Last night was fun. I'd like to spend more time with you, and as it happens, you could help me out with a certain *situation*. I was going to offer you money." He winced. "But I remembered how you reacted to that envelope of cash when I first arrived."

"Money?" Surely this wasn't what it sounded like.

"I want you to come with me to Edinburgh for a few days."

"Why?" She hesitated, realizing this was her perfect opportunity to set the record straight. "Um, Ian… Last night was a spur of the moment thing. You and I are not going to continue having…" She wasn't sure what to call that thing they had done. *Sex* seemed too blunt, but *coitus* was clinical and absurd.

He jumped on her moment of indecision. "We enjoyed a mutually satisfying intimate encounter."

"It was spontaneous," she said. "It happened. But it's not a good idea to move forward. In fact, last night was a big mistake. I'd prefer it if we go back to being acquaintances."

The #2 bachelor in all of Great Britain appeared dumfounded. Maybe he'd never had a woman walk away. "Ye don't know what ye're saying," he said, his accent thicker than usual. "Ye're not making sense. Did I offend you somehow? I know I'm not always the sharpest tool in the shed. I'll apologize for whatever stupid thing I said."

Her smile was forced. "No apologies required. Seriously. Last night was…enjoyable. We'd both had an emotional day. Things got out of hand. We're not suited to each other, though. I'd prefer not to build on something that has no future. Please understand it's not you. I'm sure some nice woman in Edinburgh will enjoy your company."

"I wasna going to pay ye for sex, ye daft woman."

"Then what was the money for?"

"To hire you as a smokescreen. Though remembering your rant when I first arrived, I thought perhaps I could donate a large sum to the charity of your choice in exchange for—"

"In exchange for what?" She was flustered and hurt that he would offer her cash after last night.

He glared. "I have to meet the queen. The place will be crawling with photographers. I thought if you went with me posing as my fiancée, word would get around, and I'd be removed from that ridiculous list."

"The queen? Of England?"

"Aye. Scotland, too."

"And you want a fiancée…"

"In name only," he said hastily. "Think of yourself as a bodyguard."

"Do you know how ridiculous this whole conversation is? Did you hit yourself on the head during last night's rescue? Do you have a fever? Why would the queen want to meet you?" She paused. "Sorry. That sounded terrible. You know what I mean."

His gaze was wry. "Believe me, I was as gobsmacked as you are when I got the word. I'm to receive an Order of the British Empire honor for my civilian contribution to Naval safety. Though traditionally a Buckingham Palace event, this year the queen will host the ceremony at Holyrood

Palace instead of London. I suppose it's a nod to the fact that we Scots voted not to leave the realm."

"I see..." Bella shook her head slightly, mostly to see if she was still asleep and dreaming. Nope. The smell of coffee and the sounds of birdsong outside the kitchen window said this was all too real. "I don't know what to say. Congratulations, Ian."

His pained reaction told her he didn't appreciate her formal response. "I would get out of it if I could, believe me. Apparently, unless I'm on my deathbed, my presence is mandatory."

"Well, of course it is. She's the queen, for heaven's sake."

"Which is why I need you for moral support. I have to get a tux. And maybe a haircut. The whole prospect gives me hives."

"Don't look at me. I'm a clueless American. I wouldn't know the first thing about accompanying a famous hero to a formal English occasion. Sorry, Ian. Count me out."

Chapter Twelve

"I'm not a hero," he insisted stubbornly. "I created a product that saves lives. The military lads and lasses who do the water rescues are the heroes."

"Whatever you say. Your modesty doesn't negate the fact that the freaking Queen of England is going to pin a medal on your chest. This is huge, Ian. You should be proud."

"It's a medallion, actually. On a fancy ribbon," he muttered. He was losing the battle. That just wouldn't do. He'd made up his mind. If he had to go put on a monkey suit and show up at the queen's residence in Edinburgh, Bella Craig was going to be at his side. It was the only idea that made the upcoming event remotely bearable.

"Fifty thousand pounds," he said desperately. "To the charity of your choice. In exchange for three days of your company."

Bella had changed since last night. Up until yesterday, he'd been learning to read her facial expressions and the emotional cues in her lovely, deep blue eyes. Now, in the cold light of day, she seemed almost a stranger. It was a peculiar transformation considering they had both been naked in each other's arms only a few short hours ago.

Frankly, it had been the best sex of his life. So much so, he'd virtually lost consciousness at the end. A mixture of exhaustion, spent adrenaline, and sexual satiation had left him comatose. Waking up alone this morning was a blow to the gut. Bella had backed away from him. Why, he didn't know.

In retrospect, she had seemed eager and responsive every step of the way. Surely she'd had an orgasm there at the end. Hadn't she?

Mortification sent heat racing from his throat to his hairline. *Holy hell.* He had no clue if Bella had climaxed or not. He'd been so ridiculously wound up from months of abstinence, desperately wanting Bella, and the residual effects of making a fool of himself with the reporters that he had completely lost his senses at the last.

No wonder she was cool and distant today. He'd coaxed her into bed and then left her high and dry.

She stood up unexpectedly and carried the pitcher of cream to the fridge, her back to him. "That's a lot of money, even for Bachelor # 2. You're being ridiculous, Ian. Either go on your own, or ask one of your scientist buddies. You said some of them are women."

"I don't want another woman," he said urgently. He went to her and wrapped his arms around her waist from behind. "Please, sweet Bella. I need you with me. I swear I do." Resting his chin on top of her head, he inhaled the scent of her shampoo.

She eluded his grasp and leaned against the sink, arms folded across her chest. "You really don't know much about the female sex, do you?"

The tart question was clearly rhetorical.

He shrugged. "I never claimed to. Are you going to tell me why you didn't linger this morning for round two?"

A spot of red appeared on each of her cheeks. Her steady gaze faltered. "I didn't know that's what you wanted."

"You could have touched me...maybe whispered in my ear," he said mildly. "And for the record, a man *always* wants round two."

"Ah." She picked up a drying cloth and twisted it between her hands. Then she shot him a sideways glance. "Here's the thing, Ian. Did it ever occur to you to simply ask me as a friend to help you out in Edinburgh?"

"Um..." He felt his throat close up, just as it always did preceding a stutter. Breathing slowly, he controlled the impulse. "I didn't know our friendship had reached that point," he said.

Bella scowled at him, distinctly un-lover-like. "We had sex last night. That's at least friends-with-benefits where I come from," she said. "Or perhaps you're too proud to ask for help? Is that the problem, Ian? Maybe it's easier to buy what you want?"

"Damn it..." Most people thought he was a pretty decent fellow. Why did Bella's unflattering estimation sting so much?

"If you want my cooperation, that's my price," she said, her gaze stormy and stubborn. "A simple request from you—no money changing hands—and the understanding that this trip would be strictly platonic. I want to be very clear about that."

"Don't worry," he grumbled. "I got the message loud and clear."

"And?"

This whole thing was working out to be a disaster. "What if I say I want to forget about Edinburgh so we can stay here and spend a week or two in bed? Together…"

Bella nibbled her bottom lip. "Not an option. I take equal responsibility for what happened last night. Don't worry about that. I learn from my mistakes, though. I like you, Ian. You're a sweet guy. If I were going to fool around with anybody, it would probably be you. I have to look at the big picture, though. You and I don't line up. I'm sorry."

The feeling in the pit of his stomach felt a lot like despair. "Fine," he said curtly. "Will you go to Edinburgh with me please, Bella? I would very much appreciate it."

She nodded slowly. It was impossible to guess what she was thinking. No Sphinx was ever more inscrutable. "I suppose it could be fun. I'll make arrangements for Cinnamon. And I'll tell Finley where I'll be. Anything else I need to know before we leave?"

He shoved his hands in his pockets and ground his teeth. "Not a thing. Not a damn thing."

* * *

Bella packed and unpacked her suitcase half a dozen times in the next seventy-two hours. She had plenty of casual clothes for exploring Edinburgh and the surrounding countryside, but nothing remotely suitable for a formal visit to Holyrood Palace in the company of Bachelor #2.

Hopefully, she would be able to find what she needed while helping Ian pick out a tux. Honestly, she was surprised he didn't already own one. Her ankle was recovering nicely, so she wouldn't have to show up in sneakers, thank goodness.

She and Ian had spent very little time together since their confrontation in the kitchen. Unfortunately, she hadn't been well-versed in how to act during an awkward morning after. Her only saving grace was that Ian still had no clue she had fled from his bed the moment after sex. A more sophisticated woman would have slept for a while, maybe tried again in the middle of the night, and been more vocal about her wants and needs.

Bella was book smart, but she was a failure as a femme fatale.

Fortunately, she had plenty of things on which to focus on other than her own shortcomings, namely her responsibilities to her brother.

Already, Finley's charming house seemed like home. Though two different local teenagers would be tending to Cinnamon in Bella's absence, there were still items to be taken care of: mail, bills, and the like.

Not to mention laundry, packing, and creating a list of all the points of interest in Edinburgh.

In between clothes shopping and the fancy ceremony, Ian had promised to play tour guide. She planned to hold him to that.

At last Wednesday morning rolled around. Ian had rescued his rental sedan from town and had it washed and filled with petrol, as he called it. All that was left was to load the car and lock up the house.

Poor Cinnamon's ears drooped and her tail wagged sadly. She had to know they were leaving. Bella crouched and scratched the dog's belly. "It's only three days, my sweet. I'll be back before you know it."

"What about me?" Ian asked, lounging in the doorway, watching her with a sharp gaze.

She stood and shrugged. "I assumed we'd part company after the ceremony. You heading on to London. Me back here."

Ian bristled. "Don't shoo me out the door yet. Finley said I could stay as long as I wanted. I'm not ready to return to London and the rat race. Portree is a delightful wee town. I barely know it yet, so I might stay the whole time you're here. Perhaps longer."

"Is that some kind of threat? I have my novel to work on. You'd be in my way." This was *her* turf. Sort of. How dare Ian Larrimore worm his way into what was left of her vacation?

Before he could answer, her cell phone buzzed in her pocket. She scowled at Ian and held up a hand. "We're not done with this conversation."

Turning her back on her tormentor, she swiped to answer the call and smiled. "Hey, Finley. What's up?"

Her brother's voice was cheerful. "Mornin', Bella. How's Portree? How's Cinnamon? How's my ornery baby sister?"

"No complaints. Is anything wrong?" She hadn't expected to hear from Finley while he was on his honeymoon…at least not often.

"Nothing serious."

Her heart sank. "What happened?"

"Well, McKenzie got food poisoning, and then about the time she felt better, the two of us accidentally fell asleep in the sun, and now she has a bad sunburn. Poor baby just wants to come home."

"Oh, no. I'm so sorry, but no worries. I'll move over to the hotel and give you your privacy."

"Absolutely not."

She had to hold the phone away from her ear. Finley's protest was loud and vehement. "You're newlyweds," she said. "This is *your* house. It wouldn't be right for me to stay."

"McKenzie and I will take it as a personal insult if you *or* Finley try to leave. I'm dead serious about this, Bella. My bride and I have had almost four weeks of wedded bliss. I think we can handle a bit of company. I'll move things around in my office and get a bed from the attic for you. There's plenty of room."

"If you're sure..." She didn't argue anymore. After a day or two, Finley would see that the sweet old house was a little *too* cozy for a man and his new wife and two extra people.

"I insist. We're planning to fly back on Friday. See you then—"

"Oh, but wait..." It was too late. Finley ended the call.

"Well, that's just peachy," she muttered.

Ian jingled his keys in his hand. "What is it?"

"Finley and McKenzie have decided to come home early. They're adamant that neither of us are expected to leave... In fact, they *want* us to stay. So I need your help for a few minutes. It won't take long. They'll be here before you and I return from Edinburgh. I need to change the sheets, and I want to have all of my stuff out of the master suite."

"Where are we taking it?" He had a funny look on his face.

"Finley says he can set up a bed for me in his office."

"You could bunk with me," Ian said.

Searching his face for evidence of humor and finding none, she smiled wryly. "I appreciate the offer, but I wouldn't want Finley to get the wrong idea. He's very protective of me."

"Surely he wouldn't insert himself into your romantic life."

"Clearly you never had a sibling. I wouldn't put it past him to lock me in my room at night. The man barely saw me for a decade, but now he relishes his new role as family patriarch."

Bella didn't wait to see if Ian would follow. She rushed past him and up the stairs. Flinging open the door to Finley's bedroom, she winced. Though most of her personal items and some of her clothes were already packed for Edinburgh, the rest of her belongings were scattered here, there, and everywhere in between.

Ian wandered in and gazed at the semi-orderly chaos of books and papers and everything else she thought she wouldn't need to meet the queen. "How the hell did you fly from North Carolina with all this?"

She started picking up books. "Go find a box in Finley's workroom, will you? I shipped my research materials before I came. When I'm working, I like to have my favorite resources at hand."

"You haven't heard of e-books?" he asked, lifting a sardonic brow.

"Sneer if you will. You have your process, I have mine."

By the time Ian returned with two cardboard cartons, she had sorted and stacked her library into like-sized piles for easier packing. Bookworms learned early in life how to move the important stuff when necessary.

He dropped the boxes on the floor. "Here you go. Call me when you're done, and I'll carry them downstairs."

"Hey, wait," she said indignantly straightening with her hands on her hips. "I thought you said you would help me."

Ian shook his head. "No. *You* said that. I didn't say anything."

"Are you pouting because I won't move in with you?"

His grin was wicked. "I don't pout, Bella. When the time comes, I know how to get what I want."

He walked out of the room, leaving Bella to stare, stunned, at the mess she had made. Stupid man. Aggravating, infuriating, oh-so-superior male. Of course she couldn't share the guest room with him. What would Finley and McKenzie think? Not to mention the fact that Bella was never going to have sex with Ian Larrimore again. Probably.

It took her just under an hour to stuff everything into the two boxes and a large plastic garbage bag she retrieved from the kitchen. After shoving the bulky containers out into the hallway with her only slightly tender foot, she summoned Finley. "All set," she yelled.

Not waiting to see if he heard her, she went to the linen closet, found a fresh set of lavender-scented sheets, and carefully made up the bed. When she was done, she smoothed the coverlet and surveyed the room. All that was left was to touch up the bathroom.

She'd heard Ian huffing and puffing in the hall as he moved her things downstairs. Since he wasn't around to make fun of her, she decided to leave a few welcoming touches for the newlyweds. Carefully folding back the covers on either side of the bed, she fetched several of her favorite handmade chocolates she'd bought from a shop in the village and arranged them on the pillows. Then she picked up the one slim volume of Emily Dickinson poetry she had saved out of the packing frenzy and set it prominently on the duvet.

Standing back to survey her handiwork, she felt a pang of jealousy. Finley was so happy, happier than she had ever seen him in his life. McKenzie brought out the best in him. He doted on her and vice versa. Even so, they still enjoyed arguing and challenging each other. They were both strong, stubborn personalities with their own way of approaching life.

Bella would like to believe there was a man out there somewhere who would be as perfect for her as Finley was for McKenzie. During brief moments over the past few days, she had thought it might be Ian.

Sadly, she no longer believed that. He was too much like her in some ways. When they both got lost in their work, they liked to be entirely isolated and alone.

That was certainly no basis for a relationship.

Ian had been clear about his desire to remain single. Objectively, she could hardly blame him. He had a wonderful career in a fascinating city surrounded by multifaceted colleagues.

Why would a man give that up for something so plebian as matrimony?

She glanced at her watch and winced. They were already an hour and fifteen minutes past their planned departure time. Was Ian one of those men who couldn't abide having travel pans uprooted?

Turns out, he wasn't. She found him waiting patiently in the living room, reading a copy of *A Tale of Two Cities* he had plucked from Finley's bookshelf. When Bella entered the room, he set the book aside and stood. "Ready to go?" he asked calmly.

Something about his manner made her jumpy. It was one thing to be here in Portree with the man. Now they were going to be spend time together in a whole new environment. "I'll pay for my own hotel room," she said. "In Edinburgh," she added, in case there was any doubt.

He shook his head. "Absolutely not. You're doing me a favor. There won't be any cost to you."

But there would be. She knew it in her heart, yet she walked out to the car anyway and climbed in beside the handsome, unusual, freakishly intelligent scientist. No matter the outcome, she couldn't let him go alone. Ian needed her, so she would be there for him.

The drive from Portree to Edinburgh took just over five hours on a good day. Fortunately, this was an even *better* day. The sun blazed down gently from a powder blue sky. Lamb-like clouds scampered across the heavens. The air was warm, but not hot. As far as Bella could tell, the weather was the kind of rare gift that made visitors to Scotland dig out their cameras.

Ian stopped multiple times, patient with her frequent exclamations of delight. With the windswept glens, majestic mountains, tiny villages with tea shops and friendly locals, the miles melted away.

It occurred to her that without Ian's trip to Edinburgh, she might never have made time to see Glen Coe or Rannoch Moor or any of the other picturesque spots they passed along the way. Certainly the prospect of driving herself over these distances was daunting.

At last, they entered the outskirts of the historic city of Edinburgh. She had read about it, studied about it, but she had never visited. Soon, she found herself incredulous that she hadn't put this historic and beautiful metropolis on her to-do list.

While Ian negotiated the traffic, Bella focused on the sights and sounds. It was clear from the outset that the city was anchored with several iconic landmarks. First and foremost was the massive Edinburgh Castle. Visible from virtually everywhere around town because of its location on the highest elevation, the castle was both impressive and daunting. It was easy to see why it had played such a pivotal role down through history.

Ian pointed out a natural feature that also held sway over the city. Arthur's Seat was a steep hilltop ringed in gorse and climbed by numerous tourists over the course of the weeks and months.

Anticipation and excitement flooded Bella's chest, momentarily obscuring her reservations about the trip. All she had to do for the next few days was to enjoy playing tourist and to stay out of Ian's bed. How difficult could it be?

Chapter Thirteen

Ian couldn't remember the last time he'd spent a more enjoyable or more frustrating day. Watching Bella "see" Scotland was a delight he hadn't anticipated. Her enthusiasm knew no bounds. She must have taken a hundred photographs before they stopped for a picnic lunch at the side of a small, unremarkable loch. Even that was deemed spectacular.

Still, underneath his enjoyment ran a deep vein of sexual frustration. His bubbly companion treated him like a favorite uncle. Nothing in her behavior suggested they had spent the previous night in his bed.

Either she was a consummate actress, or the interlude had meant nothing to her. Both choices were problematic in their own way.

He stewed about it as they drove, managing to keep his libido in check with the promise that surely he could eventually decipher the code…solve the problem. Puzzles of any kind were a welcome challenge to him. He loved utilizing his brain, shaking up the synapses and seeing if he could get extra neurons to fire.

Bella Craig wasn't a science experiment, but he was determined to dissect her cool responses this morning and get to the truth. Had she found him boring in bed? That would be a bitter pill to swallow.

Was it better to know the truth? Or should he leave the whole thing alone and *carpe diem* with the best of them?

The hotel he had chosen in Edinburgh was pricey, but known for its discretion. He'd seen no sign of photographers following him yet, but he doubted they had given up.

The elegant building combined a historic façade and interesting architectural details with amenities and accommodations tailored for the modern guest. Paying for two rooms was not the problem. What he was worried about was whether or not he had a shot in hell at convincing Bella they deserved another chance.

Everyone knew sex wasn't always great for women the first time with a new partner. It was up to him to convince her that he almost always improved with practice.

They checked in at the front desk and carried their bags up a narrow flight of stairs. The hotel did have an elevator, but it was old and finicky by the desk clerk's admission, so they avoided it. Their two assigned rooms were side by side on the third floor with a great view of the city. Though the accommodations didn't have a connecting door, Ian wasn't worried. If all went well, Bella would be spending the night with him.

She hesitated, her room key in hand. "What's the schedule?" she asked. "Do I need to change clothes?"

He grimaced. "I have to take care of getting a tux. But the good news is I made my appointment at a shop just off the Royal Mile. After I get fitted, we can play tourist as long as you want."

"The Royal Mile? I put that on my must-see list."

"I should think so. It's one of the most historic roads in all of Europe. Goes from the palace of Holyrood all the way up to the castle. We probably won't have time to tour the castle today, but there's lots more to see."

Bella's happy grin slugged him in the chest. "I'll be ready in five. I can't wait."

It was more like fifteen minutes than five before she joined him in the hallway, but he couldn't fault the results. Her neat khaki skirt and teal top were just right for a stroll in the warm afternoon sunshine.

"I called a cab," he said. "Parking is hard to find where we're headed."

In no time, the chatty driver deposited them at a narrow alley partway up the famous street in Old Town. Ian helped Bella out of the backseat, trying not to notice when her skirt rode upward, exposing a tantalizing length of thigh.

He cleared his throat. "This way," he said.

Bella followed along beside him, craning her neck to see the tops of weathered stone buildings that had stood for centuries. "I feel like we stepped back in time," she exclaimed.

"'Tis one of my favorite places," he said. "Well, at least when the tourists go home. It might be a wee bit crowded today."

"*I'm* a tourist."

The tart reminder made him grin. He tugged her hair. "Aye, lovely Bella. That you are."

"Where are we going?" she asked. The question was breathless. He slowed his pace when he realized that she was having trouble keeping up with his long stride.

"To see a childhood friend of my grandfather. Mr. Duffy is an old-school tailor, one of the last in the city. He's promised to fit me into a tux, God help him. His wife is also a seamstress. I thought she might be able to help you with a dress, if you like."

"Definitely. I wouldn't begin to know what's appropriate in this situation. I brought the only thing I have, but it's too casual, I'm sure."

* * *

Bella was totally out of her element and already regretting her pledge to accompany Ian to the ceremony at Holyrood. Back home in North Carolina, she found few opportunities to dress formally. Except for going to the theater or the opera with friends, she rarely put on a skirt. Even the little church she attended was extremely casual.

Ian appeared confident about their destination, so she tagged along behind him as the narrow side street became more clogged with passersby. The breeze tousled his thick, sun-streaked hair. He was wearing what she had come to think of as his mad scientist wardrobe. Ancient khaki pants. A conservative white button-down shirt, and on top, a soft cotton pullover in sky blue.

Despite the nondescript clothing, his classic good looks drew admiring glances from multiple women on the street. She was surprised he had decided to go out in public without some sort of disguise. Maybe he had given up on his attempt to run from the press. Oddly, now that he was making no effort to hide out, they hadn't seen a single reporter all day.

At last they paused before a wooden door flanked by a dusty six-paned window.

"I think this is it," Ian said. He opened the door and waited for her to precede him. The dimly-lit interior smelled of old books and ancient wood. Like the shops in Harry Potter's Hogsmeade, this establishment was charmingly cluttered. Shelves reached to the ceiling, filled with bolts of cloth and an assortment of thread and buttons and other items.

Bella loved it. While Ian greeted Mr. Duffy, and the two males chatted, she nosed around, wondering how long the proprietor had been in business. And what was this location *before* it became a tailor's shop?

Mrs. Duffy appeared through a curtained doorway at the back of the shop, crooking a bony finger at her spouse. "Quit bletherin', old man. Bring the children to the back so we can get started."

Bella shot Ian an amused look and mouthed, "*Children?*"

He shrugged, apparently resigned to his fate. She had yet to meet a man who enjoyed trying on clothes, much less being custom fitted.

The Duffys were interesting folk, as Bella's granny used to say. Both the tailor and his wife were petite and bent. Their age could land anywhere from eighty to a hundred, as far as she could tell. Mrs. Duffy wore a navy serge dress with sturdy lace-up brogans that supported her swollen ankles. Her husband was outfitted in heavy cotton britches and a forest green vest over a natural linen shirt. A tape measure dangled from his neck. The pockets of his vest were adorned with rows of straight pins waiting to be used.

The Duffys' accents were so heavy, Bella had to listen carefully to understand their words. The back room to which Bella and Ian had been escorted was larger than the front portion of the shop, though not by much. Large three-paned mirrors on either side of the space were one of the few semi-modern touches. Bella had seen something similar while wedding-gown shopping with a friend.

The floor was covered in Oriental rugs that were so ancient and worn the patterns were no longer discernable. Old gaslight sconces on the walls had been converted to electricity. The bulbs flickered cheerfully. All in all, the warm, old-fashioned illumination was flattering and atmospheric.

Mr. Duffy tapped Ian on the shoulder. "Take off your shirt, lad, and we'll get started."

Though Bella wanted to linger and watch the show, Mrs. Duffy tugged her elbow and steered her to the far corner of the room. "Your young man's in good hands," she said. "Let's see what we can do for you."

Though Bella did indeed need a dress, she was far more interested in what was happening with Ian. Thanks to the mirror, she was able to sneak peeks at him with no one the wiser. When he shed his sweater and pulled his shirt over his head without ceremony, she had to stifle a sigh of appreciation. Even at this distance, his torso was a thing of beauty.

Broad shoulders narrowed to a trim waist. His rib cage rippled with sleek muscle. Though his clothing choices leaned toward the ill-fitting and worn, his naked body told a far different story. Unfortunately, Mr. Duffy didn't ask his client for further disrobing. Instead, he went straight to work measuring and making notes.

Mrs. Duffy snapped her fingers in front of Bella's nose. "Quit moonin' over the lad. He's flesh and blood like the rest of 'em. He'll break your heart if you let him. Show some backbone, young Bella. Back when I was a lass yer age, I was taught that my husband would tell me what to do. I didn't think for myself. Things are different now."

"Yes, ma'am," Bella said meekly, standing completely still as the little woman did her work.

"I suppose you think I'm an old biddy who should be mindin' my own business."

"No," Bella said carefully, lifting her arms and holding them out to the side as directed. "But he's not my young man. We're just friends."

The little seamstress made a sound in the back of her throat that could have meant anything. "I may be old, but I remember what it was like when me blood ran hot. It's a fine time you'll be havin' with that strappin' lad. E'en so, make sure 'twill last before you go headfirst into the current. A broken spirit's even worse than a bruised heart."

Bella's cheeks felt fiery hot. A change in subject was in order. "What kind of dress did you have in mind for me?" she asked. The old woman, surprisingly nimble, knelt and measured the hem of Bella's simple cotton skirt as a benchmark for her work.

Mrs. Duffy lifted her head and grimaced. "Ye know, I'm sure, that this isn't New York or Paris. Ye've only to see our lovely Princess Katherine on state occasions to know that a woman can be stylish without showing a lot of skin. If ye'll trust me, I'll have that lad over there panting at your feet."

"No panting," Bella said firmly. "No feet. All I need is a modest dress to visit the palace. No one will notice me anyway. Ian is the one receiving the honor from the queen, not me."

"And the boy has asked you to go with him."

"Yes." Suddenly the reality of the situation sank in. On Friday evening, Bella was going to visit a member of the royal family in the royal castle. Her stomach knotted. Bella was a bookworm...an introvert...a woman who preferred coffee and a good novel to a party where she had to wear high heels. Why had she ever said yes to Ian's invitation?

After that, there wasn't much opportunity to talk. Mrs. Duffy measured everything there was to measure, though thankfully without Bella having to disrobe. When Bella glanced once in Ian's direction, he looked hot and flustered and uncomfortable. Poor guy. This was not his thing at all.

At last, the torture ended. Mr. Duffy nodded his satisfaction and beamed at his wife. "The two of them make a fine pair, don't they?"

Mrs. Duffy joined her husband, momentarily leaning her head against his shoulder in a gesture that tugged at Bella's heart. "Aye, that they do." She smiled at Bella. "Come back in the morning at eleven, my dear. We'll be ready for your fitting. I think you'll be pleased."

"Pleased, my ass," Ian groused as they stepped outside into the sunshine. "I'd rather walk the plank on a pirate ship." He stopped in the middle of the street and scraped his hands through his hair. "Are you sure I can't beg off? They wouldn't want me there if I'm contagious. I could tell them I have the flu…maybe even something worse."

Bella knew he wasn't talking about the fitting. "It's a huge honor, Ian. Think of it as a very impressive line on your resume." She understood his misgivings. She really did. At the moment, however, it was her job to get the reluctant genius to the palace at the appointed time. "I'm hungry," she said, trying to distract him. "Do you have any ideas for dinner?"

"I'm not a child," he said. "I have a superior IQ that is not prone to distraction. You can't placate me that easily."

The slight smile tilting his lips told her he was kidding. "Fine," she said, moving out of the throng of tourists and plopping down on a concrete bench in front of a secondhand bookstore. "Let me know when you're finished pitching a hissy fit."

He joined her on the bench. "Hissy fit?"

"What? Don't they say that in Scottish?"

"We speak the Queen's English same as you," he said wryly, tucking a stray hair behind her ear so casually it took her breath away. "But no, I haven't heard that one, though I can guess from the context that you were impugning my manhood."

The brush of his fingers against her cheek shook her to the core. *She was falling in love with him.* The realization stunned her. Ian was a loner and very happy with his life, at least once this temporary unpleasantness over the magazine article faded. He didn't show any indication of wanting a wife or kids or anything else so ordinary.

She had told herself she could enjoy his company for what it was. Superficial. Enjoyable. Temporary. For a smart woman, she had been lamentably short-sighted. Simply because Ian was a bit clueless about some things, she had made the naïve assumption she could "manage" him…or at the very least, manage their relationship on her terms.

When had she lost control of the situation?

Ian cocked his head and smiled at her quizzically. "Cat got your tongue?"

Apparently, the unwelcome bolt of clarity had shocked her into a long silence. "Um, no. I was thinking about what you said. We do speak the same language. But it sounds really different over here."

"Different bad or different good?"

She punched his arm. "Don't fish for compliments, Bachelor number two. You know how women react when you roll your *R*s."

"I've never noticed," he said soberly. His eyes danced with humor, so she didn't put much stock in his pseudo humility.

"Will you answer a question for me?" she said suddenly.

He froze...like a deer in the headlights of an oncoming car. "What kind of question?"

"Oh, relax. I'm not going to ask you to have my babies."

"Very funny. Go ahead. I'm an open book."

"What happened to your mother?"

Every bit of expression fled his face instantly, leaving him stoic and visibly closed off to her prodding. "Why is that important?"

"I don't know. Most people talk about their parents. You mentioned your father, but never said much about your mother. I'm curious."

"Curiosity killed the cat."

"In any language," she quipped. The fact that he actually chuckled loosened the knot in her stomach.

"My mother left us," he said. "When I was four. She said my father was too wrapped up in his work to pay any attention to her. She wanted to be with a man who put her first. Dad never even contested the divorce papers she filed. I think it crushed him."

"I'm so sorry."

Ian shrugged, his gaze trained on a young boy across the way playing a miniature set of bagpipes to entertain the crowd. "My father is a complicated man. I do believe he feels things deeply, but he's not really able to express his emotions. I can't imagine how he snagged my mother in the first place."

"If he looks like you, I can make an educated guess."

Ian turned so their knees touched. He took her face in his hands. "Why, Bella Craig. Was that a compliment? I'm speechless."

Without warning, he kissed her. In the middle of the Royal Mile. With tourists from around the world milling about. The sun was shining, music played in the distance. Ian's lips were firm and warm and coaxing.

It was like something out of a romantic comedy where the theme song plays and the audience knows everything is falling into place. Bella leaned closer, her hands on his shoulders, their breath mingling. His sweater beneath her fingertips was warm from the sun.

She pulled away momentarily and rested her forehead against his collarbone, trying to catch her breath. "You know you're a hunk," she said. "Don't try to be coy."

"I'm not a hunk. I'm a scientist. I'm pretty sure the two are mutually exclusive."

The deep timbre of his voice held something elusive. Reassurance perhaps? Did he know how she felt? That would be the ultimate humiliation. She could see the headlines now: *Naïve American tourist left heartbroken and alone after Highland fling with Bachelor #2.*

Shoring up her defenses, she broke away from him and pretended an intense interest in the couple arguing loudly a few steps away. "I really am hungry," she said. "What about fish and chips?"

Chapter Fourteen

Ian tossed and turned beneath the covers of his narrow hotel bed, trying to blame his insomnia on the lumpy mattress. If he were a travel writer, he'd be forced to deduct a star for his lack of sleep. Unfortunately, he knew what or who was really behind his misery. Her name was Bella, and she was no doubt sleeping peacefully on the other side of the wall.

Earlier, after buying fish and chips and consuming them at a small outdoor table, he and Bella had walked up the Royal Mile and back down, peering into shops and in general enjoying the early autumn evening. The sun dropped low in the sky, painting the historic castle in golden light.

A dozen times Ian had come close to blurting it out. *Sleep with me tonight. I want you in my bed. Say yes, Bella.* In every instance, though, he had lost his courage at the last, or something had interrupted the moment.

Bella had insisted on walking all the way back to the hotel, a distance of three miles at least. After their return, she professed exhaustion and disappeared into her own room.

Now Ian was at the mercy of his troubled thoughts. It wasn't only unsatisfied sexual hunger keeping him awake. The prospect of the ceremony at the castle hung over his head like a dark cloud of doom. He hated exposing himself in public. That's what this felt like. People staring at him. Judging him. He didn't want the award...didn't deserve it. All he yearned for was to live his life in peace and do the work he was trained to do.

Eventually, he dozed, but he slept only in snatches. When morning finally dawned, he dragged himself about of bed and used a miserably cold shower to revive himself. Afterward, he texted Bella.

Breakfast?

She must have been in the shower, too, because she didn't answer. Which meant he spent the next few minutes imagining her lush body naked and wet. Damnation. This trip to Edinburgh was going to drive him insane one way or another.

In the end, he decided not to wait for her. He needed space and time to think. Over unexceptional scrambled eggs, sausage links, and white-bread toast, he brooded. In his present mood, it seemed a mistake of monumental proportion that he'd insisted Bella accompany him to the ceremony. It was bad enough *he* had to suffer through it. Now, she would be there to witness any awkward flubs on his part. The thought made him cringe.

Bella was poised and graceful and the kind of woman who stood out in social settings. Her warm, magnolia-kissed accent. Her genuine laugh. The way she lit up when talking about a topic that interested her. It was hard to believe that no man had staked a claim.

On the other hand, she could be decidedly prickly when she wanted to be. Maybe she had kept would-be suitors at a distance.

He was finishing up a final cup of tea when the subject of his musings appeared in the dining room. She was flushed and damp and dressed in running clothes. Clearly, she had been up and out early.

"Hey," Bella said. "How are the eggs? I'm starving." Without waiting for an answer, she hastened over to the breakfast buffet and filled her plate.

He stared across the room at her indignantly, noting the way her running shorts hugged her heart-shaped bottom. Long, toned legs gave evidence of her dedication to exercise. The bounce of her thick, dark ponytail made him smile, despite his frustration.

When she joined him and began buttering her toast, he did his best to tamp down his volatile emotions. "You went for a run?"

She eyed him over her cup of juice and nodded. "It's a beautiful morning. I couldn't resist. But don't worry. I'll be dressed and ready in plenty of time for our appointment."

"Did it occur to you that I might have liked to join you?"

Her small pink tongue darted out to catch a crumb at the corner of her mouth. "I'm sorry. It was a spur of the moment thing."

He stared at her intently, cataloging each detail from her stubborn chin to her deep-as-a-mountain-lake blue eyes. "We need to talk, Bella."

Every trace of exercise-induced color leached from her face. Her gaze darted away from his, landing on the antics of two fussy toddlers nearby. "No," she said firmly. "I don't believe we do."

He reached across the table and took one of her hands in his. "Tell me the truth, Bella. When we had sex the other night, you didn't have an orgasm, did you?"

"Ian!" Her face turned a bright crimson shade somewhere between tomato-red and all-out sunburn. "You can't say things like that," she hissed. "Someone will hear you."

He lowered his voice and leaned toward her. "You're avoiding the question." He paused, his brain spinning. "That's why you left my bed," he said, only now realizing what had transpired. "And it wasn't in the morning when you woke up and ran off. You sneaked out as soon as I fell asleep. Lord, Bella. I'm sorry. Please give me another chance. I'm not usually so selfish. My only excuse is that it had been a long time for me, and I seem to lose my head around you."

If anything, his explanation made things worse. Bella looked hunted. Her fingers clenched the cutlery, her expression aghast. "I'm not doing this," she said. "Get a grip, Larrimore. I'll meet you in the lobby at a quarter 'til." Before he could stop her, she fled, leaving a third of her meal uneaten.

* * *

Bella was so humiliated she could barely look at her reflection in the mirror. As she used the small hotel hair dryer to tame her hair, she felt her face flush all over again. Somehow Ian had put two and two together and come up with the correct answer. Now she had a choice to make. She could fib and say the sex was great, and he had rocked her world. Or she could refuse to discuss the topic altogether. Last but not least of her options was to admit the truth, that she had sneaked away right after he fell asleep, not because she hadn't enjoyed herself, but because she was embarrassed and unsure.

None of the alternatives were the least bit appealing. For several long minutes she considered the possibility of simply calling a cab and hightailing it to the train station. The only thing holding her back was the thought of Ian having to endure the ceremony at the castle all on his own.

He was a grown man. There was no reason in the world for her to feel sorry for him or worry about his wellbeing. Even so, she couldn't bring herself to abandon him. Truthfully, the thought of going back to Portree without the handsome scientist made her sad. Ian was a complex and fascinating man. Being with him was stimulating in more ways than one.

When she arrived in the hotel lobby two minutes early, Ian was already waiting. He stood by the ornate fireplace, his fingers drumming restlessly on the mantel. "I'm here," she said, smoothing her hair self-consciously. She rarely wore it down, but she wanted to see what the dress would look like without a fancy updo.

He stared at her unsmiling. "In case I forgot to mention it, *I'm* paying for your dress."

"Oh, but—"

He interrupted her with a sharp gesture of his hand. "No buts. You're doing me a favor."

She didn't even try to argue. It would have been a lost cause.

For the second day in a row, they took a cab over to Old Town, presumably because Ian thought they should show up for their fitting fresh and not sweaty from walking across Edinburgh. The Duffys were waiting with smiles and sly comments about the handsome couple. Mr. Duffy took Ian off to one side of the room. Mrs. Duffy steered Bella toward the other.

The minuscule dressing room Mrs. Duffy offered so proudly barely allowed Bella to turn around, but she managed to disrobe and slide the dress over her head. Though it was not finished—the hem had to be finalized, and the sleeves as well—Bella was stunned at how the elderly seamstress had so accurately pegged her figure.

The fabric was black silk Crepe de Chine, high quality and beautifully lustrous. The dress skimmed Bella's curves flatteringly, but stayed well within the bounds of what would be considered appropriate for a palace visit. The simple scoop neck and long sleeves were modest in the extreme. The cut of the dress and the way it draped Bella's curves gave a far different impression.

A hidden side zipper snugged the dress at her waist. Black jet buttons at the wrists and at the back of the neck added a touch of glamour. Bella flung open the door and pirouetted in front of the mirror. "I love it," she said. "You're a genius." She had always rued her unabashedly feminine curves, but this dress made her look truly stylish.

While Mrs. Duffy pinned the hem and the sleeves, Bella shivered, excitement and anticipation bubbling in her veins. Despite everything that had happened, this ceremony in which Ian and others were to be honored would be a once-in-a-lifetime experience.

Mrs. Duffy looked up from her position on the floor. "Did ye bring yer high heels, lass?"

"Yes, ma'am. They're in my tote." Bella was released from her fitting long enough to rummage in the bag for the required footwear. The shoes were old but not worn…classic black pumps with a narrow heel. She felt like a kid playing dress-up when she looked in the mirror.

Mrs. Duffy stood and examined Bella's reflection, her lips pursed as she concentrated. She tugged at a shoulder seam and smoothed the bodice. "Well, lass, what do you think?"

"I adore it," Bella said. "I feel like a queen myself."

"Yer the kind of woman who's a pleasure to dress. Plenty of curves to add interest to the picture."

"Thank you for the compliment. I have to give the seamstress all the credit, though. I've never had anything fit me so well."

A tinkling bell sounded in the distance. Mrs. Duffy went to the front of the shop to deal with a customer, leaving Bella to take one last look in the mirror. It was true. She did feel special. No wonder all those Hollywood types had designers on speed-dial when it came to red-carpet events. Nothing off the rack could compare to this kind of fit and detail.

She was about to step off the raised dais and return to the dressing room when curiosity got the best of her. Moving slightly, she peeked in the mirror and caught a glimpse of Ian on the opposite side of the room. Her heart stopped for three long beats. He looked magnificent. Even in his usual attire, he was striking, but now, wearing a tailor-made tux, black cummerbund, and snowy white shirt, he was nothing short of spectacular.

Luckily for her, his attention was focused on the old man. Otherwise, Bella's face would have given her away. It was difficult to parse the emotions that curled in her stomach and gave birth to the lump in her throat. Desire. Wistfulness. Distress. Yearning. Surely somewhere in that avalanche of feelings was a strain of common sense.

It wasn't news that she had fallen hard for Ian. Back in London he had hordes of women literally chasing him down and giving him their lingerie and room keys and undying devotion. Even a man who professed not to enjoy the limelight had to be flattered by the attention, albeit reluctantly.

Before she could retreat to the tiny closet that passed as a dressing room and turn back into Cinderella, Ian half turned as if he knew she had been watching him. Their gazes clashed in the mirror. The masculine visage gave nothing away. His jaw was firm, the planes of his face taut as though indicating his bare tolerance for the formal wear and the fitting itself.

What was he thinking?

Her heart beat rapidly, her breathing shallow. What would it take to tame a man like Ian Larrimore? Was there anything in the world with the power to coax him? At this very moment he seemed almost a stranger, a younger, sexier James Bond ready to take on the world. His incredible intellect and powerful body could handle any dangerous situation.

But did he know anything about love?

Even at this distance, she felt his pull like an actual touch. She wanted to throw herself at him and beg him to be normal and boring and *hers*. That, however, was not in the cards.

It cost her, but she managed to break the visual standoff. Once in the protective confines of the changing room, she leaned against the wall and put her fist to her mouth, breathing shakily. Tears sprang to her eyes. She wanted him so badly, but she was terrified of getting hurt.

No one in her life had ever loved her the way she needed and wanted to be loved. Her father had been a selfish and controlling man. Even Finley, whom she adored, had abandoned her and fled to Scotland when she was not yet sixteen. In all fairness, his father and stepmother had treated him abominably, but still...

Bella knew what it was like to be alone. It was possible to exist in a fancy house with servants and everything a young girl could possibly want and still be achingly lonely.

What was she going to do?

At long last, the interminable fittings were complete. The Duffys promised to have the finished garments delivered to Ian and Bella's hotel the following morning, hours before the actual ceremony.

It was disorienting to step back outside into the bright sunlight after spending time in the dim confines of the tailor shop. Neither she nor Ian spoke as they began to stroll up the hill. They stopped momentarily along the way and bought meat pies and sodas from a street vendor.

The awkward silence continued even after they purchased tickets for the castle tour. Once they arrived at the gate, Ian faced her soberly. "Perhaps you'd like to explore on your own?"

She shook her head, searching his eyes for answers to the questions that troubled her. "No. I'll stay with you. I've always heard it makes sense to tour with a local."

He shrugged. "I'm not exactly a local, but I've definitely been here a few times. If I go overboard with the history stuff, feel free to rein me in... I tend to go on and on when I get on a roll."

"No such thing as too much history," she said stoutly. "You forget what I do."

Fortunately for the awkward ambiance that had sprung up between them, the presence of numerous tourists made personal conversation impossible. Instead, Ian was as good as his word.

The castle was much larger than Bella had realized. Within its walls was a city in miniature. The views from the ramparts were amazing.

Though a scientist by trade and training, Ian knew as much or more than Bella did about the history of his own country. They toured the great hall, saw the crown jewels—the oldest in the British Isles—and photographed each other with the cannons of the famous Half Moon Battery. They even paused to witnessed the firing of the one o'clock gun which Bella had come to know was an Edinburgh tradition.

When they were ready to take a break from the sunshine, Ian led her to a weathered rock structure near the center of the complex. "You'll like this, I think," he said. "It's the oldest surviving building in all of Edinburgh."

They stepped through the low, arched doorway of the stone building into a small, narrow chapel. Immediately, peace and serenity enfolded them. Pale lemon light glowed from sconces on the plaster walls.

"It's beautiful," Bella whispered softly. For the moment, none of the throng of tourists outside disturbed them.

Ian's voice echoed, even though his words were quiet. "The chapel was built in the early twelfth century by David I to honor his mother, Margaret. She was an English princess, but she and her family were forced to flee from England to Scotland following the Norman invasion. By all accounts she was a pious and beloved woman. When Robert the Bruce destroyed Edinburgh Castle roughly two hundred years later, he spared St. Margaret's Chapel, and here it stands."

"How extraordinary." Bella wandered closer to the altar, trying to imagine the nine hundred years that had passed and all the souls who must have sought refuge within these walls.

Ian joined her at the braided rope that kept visitors at a safe distance. Fresh flowers scented the alcove. "The chapel is tended by a special guild whose members keep an eye on things. They also supply the flowers. Everyone in the guild is named Margaret, either first name, or middle."

When Bella sucked in an audible breath, Ian gave her a quizzical glance. "What did I say?" he asked.

She smiled at him, feeling off-kilter and amazed. "My middle name is Margaret. I never told anyone when I was growing up, because I always hated it. Seemed old-fashioned and old-lady-ish."

"I think it's a lovely name," Ian said. "Arabella Margaret Craig."

Bella winced and sighed when a family of five tromped through the door talking loudly. "After today, I'll wear my name proudly," she said. "Thank you for the tour, Ian."

They stepped aside to let the newcomers read the plaques and make a quick circuit of the small space. Fortunately, the trio of preteen boys was more interested in armaments than religious relics. Their parents led them away, leaving Bella and Ian alone once again.

Her companion seemed preoccupied now. "Any other tidbits I should know before we leave?" she asked lightly.

Ian shrugged. "I'm told they have weddings here…and baptisms. This room wouldn't hold many, though. I suppose most people are interested in the view outside."

"Not me," Bella said. "Think how perfect and intimate this would be." Especially for someone who had dedicated her adult life to studying courtship and marriage in Europe.

Yet another group of tourists intruded on the simple, quiet spot, forcing Bella and Ian to give up and leave.

Ian put on his sunglasses once they were outside. "We've pretty much seen all there is to see. Let's head back, if that's okay with you. I've made reservations at a special restaurant tonight. I hope you like French cuisine."

"Sounds wonderful," Bella said, feeling her spirits lift. She had made up her mind. There would be no rehashing of their one and only intimate encounter. As far as she was concerned, all that mattered was the here and now. They would enjoy Edinburgh as friends.

Chapter Fifteen

Ian fought a losing battle. He had tried pretending Bella was nothing more than an old friend, perhaps a favored cousin. Nothing worked. All he could think about was getting her naked and into his bed.

Serving as tour guide at the castle had tested his patience. She was so damned passionate and adorable when she got excited about history. The more questions she asked, the more he tried to entertain her. And in between, he fought the urge to snatch her up and kiss her senseless.

There had even been a split second in the chapel when he flashed on an image of him sliding a ring on Bella's finger. Holy hell. Where had that come from?

His torture had started with her skimpy running clothes at breakfast, escalated at the sight of her amazing body in the simple black dress, and reached full tilt while escorting her around the romantic castle.

He needed a break. He needed to clear his head. He needed to get away from her. ASAP.

"Shall I call a cab?" he asked, his voice hoarse and raspy.

Bella beamed. "Oh, no. Let's walk again. I love this city."

The torture continued.

As they made their way down the Royal Mile, Bella was drawn to one after another of the charming shops along the way. She bought gifts for Finley and McKenzie and a couple of smaller remembrances for girlfriends back in North Carolina. But soon, she stopped abruptly in front of a bay window with an elaborate collection of jewelry on display.

The placard, lettered in calligraphy, "Pieces Inspired by the Outlander Series."

"We can go inside, if you want to," he said, resigning himself to another half hour of cooling his heels.

Bella shook her head wistfully. "No. I hardly ever go anywhere I'd wear something that fancy."

"What's with all the amber?" he asked.

She looked at him as if his IQ was in question. "The second book is called *Dragonfly in Amber.* I thought everybody in Scotland knew that."

He held up his hands. "Sorry. A bit outside my scope. I'm more of a Grisham fan. Or Stephen King."

"You don't know what you're missing."

He grinned inwardly. She was miffed and insulted. The truth was, he was trying to get a rise out of her. He had read the first three Outlander books a year ago on the recommendation of a friend and found them fascinating. Not entirely his cup of tea, but impressive nevertheless. As a Scotsman, he'd been drawn in by the story and curious to see where the author would go next.

He tapped her arm. "If you're not going inside, can we please go back to the hotel? I'd like to take a shower, and I need to check in with a couple of my colleagues."

"Fine. Let's go. The jewelry is probably too expensive anyway."

* * *

Fortunately for his plans later in the evening, Bella loved the restaurant he had chosen. It was small and intimate with white linen tablecloths and tiny crystal vases filled with purple heather. They both chose the beef bourguignon, on the recommendation of the waiter, and were not disappointed.

The place was packed even on a weeknight, a sure testament to good food. Ian loved his homeland, but he had no illusions about Scottish cuisine. The way to a woman's heart was a classic Parisian meal topped off with fresh strawberry tarts covered in Chantilly cream.

After her second glass of wine, Bella switched to coffee. "I'm stuffed from dinner, and my head is spinning already."

He grinned lazily. "Maybe I could make your head spin."

"Stop that," Bella said. She looked sleepy and sated. Warm and happy, too.

"Stop what?"

"You know," she said. "Flirting. I told you. We're just friends."

"Ah. So you say."

"Bite me."

It was clear she wanted to be indignant, but she was too mellow to work up much steam. She wore the same khaki skirt from yesterday, this time with a royal blue cashmere sweater in deference to the cool evening. Ian thought she looked good enough to eat with a spoon.

"Hold still," he said gruffly. Leaning forward, he rescued a small dollop of whipped cream from her chin and popped it into his mouth. "Delicious."

Bella gazed at him hazily, perhaps unaware that her pupils were dilated and her soft pink lips quivered. "I won't sleep with you," she said firmly. "You are you, and I'm me, and ne'er the twain shall meet."

He leaned back in his chair and grinned, lifting a hand to summon the waiter for their check. "You're a hard woman Arabella Margaret Craig. Did it ever occur to you that I don't want my heart broken either?"

She blinked. "Who said anything about hearts?"

"Isn't that why you're keeping me at arms' length? You're afraid of love?" He tossed it out there as a dare to see what she would do.

"I'm not afraid of anything," she snapped. "Maybe I just don't want to be bamboozled by a handsome, nerdy scientist."

"Bamboozled? Really?" Her vocabulary was a hoot. On the other hand, she *had* called him handsome, so that was something.

"Men are allergic on principle to domestication. There's a reason you're a bachelor. I pity the woman who falls in love with you."

"You have me all figured out, don't you?" he said, resting his elbow on the table and leaning his chin on his hand. "We should go," he said huskily. "There's a queue outside. Someone will want our table."

She finished her coffee. "Are you always so considerate, Mr. Larrimore?"

He caught her hand in his and entwined their fingers. "Apparently not. It seems I was dreadfully neglectful of a certain woman's pleasure a few nights ago. I'd like to remedy that."

Bella lifted her nose and stood up, wobbling only slightly. "I have no idea what you're talking about."

They made their way through the maze of closely packed tables and out into the crisp, cool night. Bella leaned against the wall and took a deep breath. "Plying me with rich French cuisine to seduce me is a low trick, Ian."

He held up both hands. "You've got it all wrong. I'm going to wait for you to seduce me." He curled a hand behind her neck and pulled her close. "My new strategy is playing hard to get." With a rough laugh, mostly directed at himself, he found her mouth with his and dove in, letting the sharp, wicked pleasure roll through his veins like an electric shock.

She was pliant in his embrace, too pliant at first. "You're insane," she mumbled, kissing him back anyway. Her body was soft and warm against his. She curled her arms around his neck. "I would never give you the time of day. Women don't beg. It's unladylike."

He nipped her bottom lip with his teeth, perhaps harder than he meant to. Bella's groan went to his gut and hardened his sex so fast he shuddered. "Never is a long time." It occurred to him suddenly that they were putting on a show, even though it was mostly dark by now. "Start walking, Margaret. Before we get arrested."

Their hotel was two blocks up and three blocks over. He kept his arm around her waist as they strolled, trying his damnedest to decide what to do. He'd been kidding about the hard-to-get thing, but the more he thought about it the more he realized it was the only way to win her trust.

Hell. Being a genius was a pain in the ass sometimes.

On the corner across from the hotel, he leaned her against a lamppost and kissed her again. "Beg me to come to bed with you," he demanded.

Bella moved her head from side to side, her lips full and pouty from his attentions. "I can't. You're dangerous."

"I'm not," he swore. He deepened the kiss. She tasted like sweet cream and dark desire. He slid a hand beneath her sweater and found the tightly furled bud beneath her lacy bra. "Say it, Bella. Tell me what you want."

Her entire body trembled. "You, damn it. I want you, Ian. Are you happy now?"

The words electrified him. He wanted to scoop her up in his arms and carry her across the threshold of the hotel…which for a man who hated to cause a scene was quite a role reversal.

"You make me weak, Bella. I don't much like the feeling." It was as honest as he'd ever been with her.

"Nobody's holding a gun to your head." She caught his earlobe between her teeth and gave it a sharp bite. "Walk away. I dare you."

"Bloody hell." Insanity. That's what it was. He felt like a man possessed. Feverish. Incoherent. "Come with me."

He took her wrist in a firm grip, prepared to drag her across the street. Suddenly, a barrage of lights flashed in their faces.

"Can we have a statement, Mr. Larrimore? Who's the pretty lady? Are you still Bachelor number two, or are your days numbered?"

* * *

Bella had never actually been afflicted with a hangover. Nor was she now. But she hadn't slept worth a damn. She rolled over to sit up on the side of the bed and whimpered when the jackhammer inside her head picked up speed. "Oh, dear heaven."

She remembered the night before. Unfortunately. The wonderful bits were pretty damned wonderful. But the embarrassing denouement...

Bloody hell, as Ian would say when pushed to the edge. He had definitely been pushed to the edge last night. The more she thought about what happened, the less it made sense. The whole purpose behind Ian's bringing her with him to Edinburgh was to convince the paparazzi that he was no longer eligible for the much-touted bachelor list. She was supposed to pose as his fiancée so the piranhas would circle back and attack some other poor man.

The moment had finally come, but Ian had bolted, dragging her along behind him like a rag doll. Hotel security halted the photographers at the door, leaving them frustrated and belligerent. Ian, on the other hand, lost all reason. Instead of the romantic evening she could have sworn they were headed for, he took her to her room, opened her door, and shoved her inside with nothing more than a muttered good night.

She had tossed and turned for hours, finally falling asleep around three a.m. Likely, she'd be asleep still if an annoying shaft of sunlight hadn't peeked through the crack in the drapes this morning and stabbed her skull.

After stumbling to the bathroom like an old woman, she rummaged in her toiletry case and found the ibuprofen. She opened her mouth and washed down three tablets with tap water.

Her reflection was almost as bad as her headache. She found two very distinct hickeys at the base of her throat. Her mascara was smudged into panda eyes, and her hair had tripled in size during the night.

Dear Lord, please let me die now.

She couldn't face Ian. It was as simple as that. If the two of them went out together, they would be pinned down again. The prospect galvanized her into action. The original plan for today was a hike up Arthur's Seat. She still wanted to go, but without Bachelor #2. All she had to do was wear a baseball cap and sneak out the back of the hotel.

Leaving Ian to his fate seemed cold, but she had to think of the big picture. Tonight's ceremony was non-negotiable. She was going to have to wear the beautiful new dress, smile her ass off, and pretend that everything was all right. Until then, Ian was on his own.

After the fastest shower on record, she put on a pair of jeans, sneakers, and a navy jersey pullover. Definitely touristy. With a huge pair of sunglasses, no one would suspect her of being connected to the high-profile bachelor.

She stuffed some pound notes into her pocket, grabbed her phone, and headed down a back staircase. The kitchen manager looked at her oddly when she made her way around three cartons of lettuce and asked for the exit, but he directed her anyway.

Moments later, she slowed her mad dash to a stroll and tried to look inconspicuous. Her strategy worked. No one even glanced her way as she eased around the corner of the hotel and headed down the hill. She walked toward Old Town at a brisk pace, despite her aching head.

She was headed for Holyrood and beyond to the park. The castle was open to tourists the majority of the year, though not when the queen was in residence, which meant not today. It was an odd feeling to know that in a few short hours, Bella would be entering those imposing gates with Ian.

The park was a popular spot, but not everyone attempted the climb to the top. Bella's headache finally eased off. She relished the exertion of tackling the famous hill. There were no trees near the top, nothing like a park back home, but yellow gorse bloomed in profusion everywhere. First the road, and then a narrow path led in circles up and up.

At the end, stone steps with no handrail accessed the final ascent. She was forced to pay attention to where she placed her feet or risk a nasty fall. Huffing and puffing a bit more than usual, she finally made it all the way to the top. Edinburgh sprawled at her feet with the castle and the palace easily recognizable in the distance. From this vantage point, the Royal Mile was even more impressive. To have stood the test of time and the ravages of war was no small feat.

A geological marker at her feet gave the elevation in meters. She was too tired to care about the conversion. She perched on a convenient rock and tried to catch her breath.

Slowly, the breeze and the sunshine restored her equilibrium. She tried her best not to think about the more titillating portions of last night, but it was impossible. Even now, she could feel Ian's lips on hers, the slight rasp of his chin scraping her tender skin when he nibbled his way down her neck.

If the paparazzi hadn't shown up, would she even now be in Ian's bed?

She didn't know whether to be relieved or disappointed that their romantic night had ended in ruins. The angel on her shoulder said things had worked out for the best. The less benign alter ego pointed out that she had been seconds away from throwing all her good sense to the four winds.

Wryly, she considered the fact that Ian Larrimore had—in fact—made her beg. Perhaps the knowledge should have been humiliating, but it wasn't. He had needed her as much or more, and hadn't bothered to hide his arousal and his desperation. Her knees pressed together instinctively.

She wanted him. Badly.

As if her heated thoughts had conjured him up out of thin air, Ian's head popped up over the crest of the hill. "Hey, there," he said. "I thought I might find you here." He had accessed the top from the opposite side.

He sat down beside her and kissed the top of her head. "I feel like hell," he said, his tone conversational.

"Me, too. How did you get out of the hotel?"

"I bribed a deliveryman to hide me in his truck and give me a ride to the bottom of the hill."

"Ingenious."

"Thanks. I thought so."

"I take it the reporters were still out front."

He nodded glumly. "Oh, yes."

"I thought you were going to introduce me as your fiancée. That *was* the plan...right?"

"Yep."

"So what happened?"

"I was a wee bit off my game what with you begging me to have sex and all."

"I did *not* beg."

He bumped her shoulder with his. "Aye, lass. You did. A man remembers a thing like that."

"Why aren't you in bed sleeping off your hangover?"

"'Twas only wine, ye daft girl. A Scotsman's weaned on whiskey. It would take a lot more than last night to get me sozzled."

"I see."

Actually, Bella didn't see anything at all. She was completely and unequivocally confused. About herself. About Ian. About the hazy future.

They sat there for the longest time, not speaking at all. It was a comfortable silence. Peaceful. Almost like the feeling she'd had in the small chapel.

Groups of hikers appeared, took pictures, and made their way back down. Ian offered his services to most of them, except for the ones determined to take selfies. Bella sat and meditated in the hot sun.

Gradually, her stomach and her head recovered enough to realize she was actually hungry. When she said as much, Ian produced two packets of cheese crackers from the pocket of his jacket. "Here ye go. Never let it be said that I let a woman go hungry."

"My hero."

It would have been nice if they could have stayed up here forever. Down below awaited all sorts of beasts. Manic paparazzi. A super important ceremony in an actual castle with an actual queen.

And then there was the question of whether or not Ian and Bella would end up in bed tonight. Their track record wasn't great to this point.

He flipped her ponytail and leaned back on his hands. "Made any progress on your dissertation topic? Or your novel?"

Trust the dratted man to hit on the one glaring problem with her sojourn in Scotland. "Not exactly. I've futzed around with an outline. What would you say if I told you I was thinking about walking away from the doctoral program?"

"Aren't you finished with all the course work?"

"Yes."

"So only the dissertation?"

"Yes."

He shrugged. "Kind of a waste, don't you think? With the degree you could always teach down the road. Insurance, if you will."

She'd been hoping he would tell her to follow her bliss. "I have a mental block about it. All I want to do is work on my novel."

"Hmm…"

That was annoying. The vague syllable could mean anything. "You enjoy your work, right?"

"Of course I do."

"So shouldn't I do the one thing that gives me joy?"

He gave her a wry, somewhat fatigued grin. "I fear this is a test, and one I haven't studied for."

"Should I point out that you just ended a sentence with a preposition?"

"I'm getting a very important award tonight. I'd think you might show me a bit of respect."

"In your dreams." She linked her hand with his, and leaned her head on his shoulder. "Did I really beg? I was hoping that was a nightmare."

"You begged, lass. I was there."

Chapter Sixteen

Ian was lightheaded with relief and exhaustion. After last night, he'd been halfway expecting to find out that Bella was on a train bound for Inverness. This morning he'd had to slip the housemaid a twenty pound note along with a cajoling smile to let him peek in Bella's room and reassure himself that her belongings were still there. That had been step one.

Making it out of the hotel unseen was next.

Holding Bella in his arms again would be number three. For now, though, it was enough to feel her hand in his and know he hadn't screwed up so badly she had given up on him.

"You should do it," he said suddenly.

Bella yawned. "Do what?"

"Write your novel. To hell with being sensible."

"If that's supposed to be a pep talk, you suck at it. Finley was the designated screw-up in our family over the years. My job was to be the perfect kid. Being sensible is encoded in my DNA."

"Finley seems to have landed on his feet rather nicely. Perhaps it's your turn to be wild and free."

"I don't think people can truly change. I am who I am. I did inherit some money, though, when my father passed…Finley and I both. I *could* take a break from university life and not endanger my financial future."

"There you go. Problem solved."

She jumped to her feet. "You engineer types drive me nuts. Life isn't neat and tidy. You can't shove every problem into a box and slap a label on it."

"Are you trying to pick a fight, Bella?" He held up his hands in the universal gesture of surrender. "I'm on your side, I swear."

She scrunched up her face and rubbed her forehead. "Sorry," she muttered. "I'm in a bad mood, I guess."

"Hangover?"

"Hardly. I've never indulged to that extent."

He gaped at her. "Really?"

"Yep." She sat back down. "I told you I was the sensible one."

"Poor baby. I suppose this is all my fault."

"I'm sorry the paparazzi showed up." Bella's sympathy made him squirm inwardly.

He shrugged. "I should be used to it by now."

"You're not shy. I know about the stuttering thing, but it's more than that, isn't it? It's as if the reporters have some power over you. I don't understand it entirely. Do you, Ian? Or is it more of a knee-jerk reaction?"

Well, here it was. Did he tell her the truth? "You're very perceptive." It wasn't an answer to her question.

Evidently, Bella took his equivocation as a rebuff, because she stood up and brushed off the seat of her pants. "I'm going to head back," she said casually. "I want plenty of time to get fancied up for tonight."

He reached for her wrist and missed. "Not so fast. I'll come with you."

She ignored him and started walking. The first eighth of a mile was precarious. No opportunity for anything but the careful descent. Eventually, the path was wide enough they could walk side by side.

Bella stayed with him physically, but she had withdrawn mentally. She hadn't misunderstood what just happened. He had tried to keep her out of his messy past, and she was hurt. Damn it. A man didn't like opening a lot of those painful boxes Bella had mentioned.

"Okay, I'll tell you," he muttered.

She stopped dead in the middle of the path and put her hands on her hips. "Forget it. I don't care." Her gaze was stormy.

Cupping her face in his hands, he kissed her softly. "I'm sorry. I'm not in the habit of airing my dirty laundry. Cut me some slack, please. The thing is…" His throat closed up. Hell. Why did Bella always have to see him at his worst?

He inhaled and exhaled. "She was a drug addict," he said bluntly, releasing Bella and continuing to walk down the hill with her at his side. "A bad one. She was miserable and unhappy, so popping a pill helped her forget. I told you my mother ran away. That part was true. What I didn't say was that my father took her name off all the accounts when he realized what she was doing with their money. After that, she actually started turning tricks…anything to get high. We lived in a small town. My father was a prominent citizen. The newspapers had a field day with the story. Everyone at school knew. It was a living hell."

"So when the reporters chase you now, it brings it all back."

"Aye. It does."

"Are you worried someone will dig up the old story?"

"It's crossed my mind. My mother lives at a long-term care facility in Glasgow. She totally destroyed her health, both mental and physical. I suspect she probably had psychiatric issues that went untreated for years. My father will care for her financial needs until the day he dies, though they haven't been legally married for years."

"But she wanted more from him."

"More than he could give, yes. I'm afraid I'm too much like him when it comes to intimacy."

Conversation dwindled to a minimum after that. Bella didn't say much. Was she wondering if he had inherited his mother's temperament? Or his father's? In either case he was no bargain.

By the time they made it back to the hotel, there was no need for subterfuge. The reporters had abandoned ship, perhaps deciding to cover the evening's festivities at the castle instead of trying to catch Ian out on the town. In the lobby, people milled about. A tour group had arrived and was checking in.

"What time do I need to be ready?" Bella asked.

"They're sending a car for us at 6:30. I thought we could nip out for a quick meal at five and then come back to change into our other clothes."

Bella shook her head. "I think I'll get room service. I'll be right here at 6:25, I promise. Don't worry. I won't make you late."

* * *

Three hours later, Ian untied his bow tie for the third time and stared in the mirror as he maneuvered the tricky knotting process. His brow was damp and his stomach churned. Bella might have ordered room service, but *he* hadn't been able to eat a bite. He'd be lucky not to barf on his shoes while he was standing in line waiting for the queen to speak to him.

At last, he was ready. Wallet. Check. Room key. Check. He even had a condom in his wallet just for the hell of it. Maybe if he could fantasize about having sex with Bella in Holyrood Palace, it would take his mind off other less enjoyable matters.

When he loped down the stairs and spotted his date for the evening, his heart stumbled. He paused on the landing to catch his breath. Bella hadn't noticed him yet. Mrs. Duffy deserved a dozen roses for knowing exactly what was appropriate for tonight's ceremony. The black dress was sexy but still demure. The hem hit right at the top of the knee, baring Bella's beautiful legs. Until this morning at breakfast, he hadn't realized quite how spectacular those legs were. His prickly American friend was the epitome of class and elegance.

With a quick glance at his watch, he straightened his tie one last time, and told himself it was going to be a great evening.

He almost believed it.

Bella looked up and smiled at him when he approached.

"You look amazing," he said gruffly. He wanted to bundle her back upstairs and keep her all to himself.

"Thank you. I hate to add to your healthy ego, but you look pretty darn good yourself." Her blue eyes were clear, no hint of anything troubling her. Good. Perhaps his confession hadn't done lasting damage.

"Shall we go?" He held out his arm, feeling like an adolescent on prom night. In the car, he outlined the evening. "I don't think we get to sit together. The honorees will be up front. But you'll be in the special VIP section, and during the reception afterward, I'll have a chance to present you to the queen."

"Present me?" Bella's voice went up an octave.

"Not like that," he said, grinning. "No curtsies."

"Thank God." She touched his knee lightly, sending a bolt of heat through his body, though he was sure she didn't mean anything sexual by it. "Ian?"

He covered her hand with his. "Yes?"

"When and how do we deal with your paparazzi? That's why I'm here. I don't want to say the wrong thing."

Something about that irritated him. "I don't know. I was going to make it up as we go along."

"'Cause you've done so well with that up until now…"

Her sarcasm made him laugh. "Fair enough. Honestly, though, I doubt we'll have to deal with it going in. There are guards at the gate, and we'll be admitted that way."

"No press inside?"

"I didn't think of that…maybe. Still, those would be more serious journalists. Surely they wouldn't care about the list thing."

"Denial. Table for two. Don't be naïve, Ian. You've won a major award. You're meeting the queen. Tonight's ceremony is big news. If you're smart, you'll have a sound bite ready."

"Maybe I should hire you as my communications director."

"Not in a million years. I'm an introvert, remember? The only difference between me and you is that I'm a nobody, and I like it that way."

"Very funny."

* * *

Bella wasn't joking, not really. She was definitely glad that Ian was the one who had to handle the limelight. Her role was to sit in the background until he wanted to use her as arm candy in his quest to get off the bachelor list.

All else aside, she was deeply moved to be entering the grounds of the famous castle. Nothing in the good old USA could compare to the centuries of history on this side of the ocean. In her head she tried to name the men and women who had walked the halls of Holyrood. The roster was staggering.

Their car pulled around in front of the castle and joined the queue waiting to enter. Palace guards flanked both side of the massive, ornate gates. At last, it was Ian and Bella's turn. They presented their credentials and were waved through. Moments later, the driver deposited them in front of a doorway where men and women dressed in formal wear made their way inside the palace.

Ian helped Bella out of the car. "Some other time if you're visiting Finley, you should come back to Edinburgh and see all of Holyrood when it's open to the public. The gardens are stunning, and as a history buff, you would enjoy the narrated tour." He paused just before they stepped inside. "That section to our left is the ruins of the original abbey."

Bella tried not to act like a country bumpkin in the big city as she was escorted through the entrance. She was actually standing inside a palace. Everywhere she looked, incredible artwork and architectural details jumped out at her. Soon, pleasant men and women in matching clothing, ushers presumably, began handing out thick vellum programs and seating the guests. Bella was lucky. Her gilt chair was at the end of a row with a clear view of the dais and the semicircle of seats where the honorees were assigned.

She squeezed Ian's hand. "Try to enjoy yourself," she said. "This is a night to remember."

He squared his shoulders, but managed a tight grin. "That's the way somebody described the Titanic's fate, isn't it?"

"You're a riot. Go on," she said. "And don't be a smart ass. I'll see you afterward."

While she waited for the remainder of the attendees to be seated, she flipped through the very formal program which included a condensed history of the palace. Mary, Queen of Scots, was one of Holyrood's most famous residents. Queen Victoria was very fond of the Scottish palace as well. Tonight's assemblage was seated in the largest room in the castle, the Great Gallery.

The ceremony commenced at the stroke of seven. The program was long but fascinating, beginning with music from a stringed ensemble that included a massive harp. After that, a series of introductions and welcome to dignitaries. At last, it was time for the awards.

The expertise of the dozen recipients ran the gamut from medicine to the performing arts to philanthropy and various fields of science. Only one person was not present, because he was in Africa dealing with refugee issues. The honorees were listed alphabetically in the program, thus placing Ian squarely in the middle. Bella waited impatiently as the first five had their moment in the sun. Then it was Ian's turn.

The queen looked diminutive standing alongside Ian. She spoke with charm and dignity about his accomplishments. Then on cue, he bent his head and she placed the beribboned medallion around his neck.

Bella had applauded dutifully after each award was presented, but this time was different. This one was personal. She beamed as Ian returned to his seat. At the last moment before he sat down, his gaze caught hers across the distance separating them. His head gave a quick bob. He was glad she was there.

It was enough for the moment.

At the conclusion of the festivities, the crowd adjourned to the far end of the Great Gallery, but the movement was carefully orchestrated. Beautifully presented hors d'oeuvres on silver trays were spread out on a succession of linen-draped tables. Two champagne fountains, both silver and undoubtedly antiques, served the thirsty guests.

Bella wanted to make her way to Ian, but he was surrounded by well-wishers. In the meantime, she grabbed a glass of bubbly so she would have something to do with her hands. Her small black evening purse hung from a narrow strap over her shoulder.

With time to kill while Ian did his thing, she studied the enormous room with interest. Its signature feature was the collection of paintings encircling the gallery, one hundred and ten in all, documenting the monarchs of Scotland going all the way back to Fergus I in 300BC. The royal highnesses were a motley crew. Young and old. Hearty and sickly. Male and female. Not all of them had lived here, of course. The palace was not built until the sixteenth century.

Her interest in the past waned abruptly when a warm male hand grasped her elbow. "Finally," Ian said. "I've been trying to get close to you for half an hour. Do you want to grab some food?"

They decided to share one plate of hors d'oeuvres. He fed her strawberries and laughed when her chin ended up covered in juice. Primly, she dabbed herself clean with a napkin. "You acquitted yourself admirably with the queen, Mr. Larrimore. Nicely done."

"Thank God I didn't have to say much." He took a sip of her champagne without asking. The casual intimacy of the moment made her stomach curl in a good way.

Handsome seemed a nondescript word to describe him. The classic lines of his profile were ruggedly masculine. Though tailored for his tall frame, the tuxedo seemed almost straining to accommodate the width of his shoulders.

Unfortunately, their intimate tête-à tête lasted barely more than ten minutes. One of the award committee members commandeered Ian and led him away. Moments later, Bella's mouth fell open when she saw Prince Harry conversing with her date.

The invited press in the room were quick to notice the unique opportunity. Bachelor #1 and Bachelor #2, side by side. Photo ops didn't get any better than that. Fortunately, Ian hadn't noticed the cameras yet. The photographers were subtle in their attentions.

When Ian beckoned her, she wound her way through the crowd, telling herself not to say something dumb. Fortunately, the prince was funny and relaxed. He won Bella's approval by praising Ian's contribution to naval rescues.

The moment was, of course, brief. Everyone wanted an opportunity to rub shoulders with royalty, particularly the red-haired, younger prince.

Ian grabbed two more glasses of champagne from a passing waiter and laughed at Bella. "You've got stars in your eyes. Should I be jealous?"

"He's so sweet and down-to-earth. I can't believe he hasn't found his own happily-ever-after."

"Not all men want marriage," Ian said. "Perhaps he's enjoying his life too much to settle down with one woman. Either that or he doesn't want to parade his private life out in public."

The offhand statement depressed Bella. Was Ian trying to tell her something without hurting her feelings? His comment about marriage could be general or personal. She hoped it was the former.

Then it struck her. She was writing a tale in her head that was more fiction than fact. In the midst of the glamor and the champagne and the storybook evening, she had begun to regard Ian as hers. That was a sure recipe for pain and heartbreak. Besides, they weren't even compatible in bed. That didn't bode well for any kind of relationship at all.

She might as well suck it up and face the truth. Ian had a life in London that didn't include her and likely never would. Their paths had crossed thanks to Finley, but that was more accident than destiny.

After meeting Harry, the Queen's quiet greeting half an hour later was almost anticlimactic. Bella nodded and murmured her gratitude for a wonderful evening. Ian repeated something similar. Then Elizabeth moved on to the next group of guests.

Ian rolled his shoulders and yawned behind his hand. "I think we can go now. I'd like to get out of these clothes."

"Of course," Bella said calmly, trying not to think about Ian Larrimore naked. "I'm ready when you are."

They headed toward the exit, but Ian was caught at the last minute by one of his fellow honorees. "I'll wait in the anteroom," Bella whispered. It was far cooler, and unlike the gallery, there were benches along the wall where she could perch and rest her aching feet.

Nothing prepared her for what happened next. One moment she was sitting quietly with her eyes closed imagining what it must have been like to attend a royal ball several centuries ago. The next instant, the twenty-first century present intruded rudely.

"May we have a statement, ma'am? You're Ian's Larrimore's date tonight, aren't you?"

Chapter Seventeen

Her eyelids flew open. The surprise was a punch to the gut, leaving her breathless with anxiety. "Ummm…"

Obviously the first question was rhetorical, because a second reporter pressed on. "May we have your name?"

"Bella. Bella Craig." There was no point in evading them. They surrounded her now, eight of them in all, two deep.

"How long have you known Mr. Larrimore?"

Her brain raced madly. Why hadn't she and Ian come up with a script for this very situation? How was she supposed to know what he wanted her to say? Damn it, where was he?

She straightened her spine and summoned a smile. "For some time," she said. Surely that was vague enough.

"Are you romantically involved?"

"Gentlemen," she said, "a lady doesn't like to tip her hand."

Oddly, there wasn't a woman in the group. Perhaps the seasoned veterans snagged all the plum assignments. All of the press here tonight were fifty plus, and they had the tenacity of hardened beggars.

Her coy comment made them laugh, but they didn't give up. A tall, gangly man who reminded her of Ichabod Crane, leaned in. "How does it feel to be with Britain's number two bachelor? Can you tell us how you snagged him? What does a woman need to lasso a man like Larrimore? How did he pick you out of the crowd?"

"Th-that's enough." Ian's stern warning rescued her just in time. She was about to lambast the rude, sexist inquisitor when her escort's deep, gravelly voice drove home the point. "L-leave her alone."

Flooded with gratitude and relief, she jumped up and latched on to his arm. She whispered in his ear, "Shall we tell them I'm your fiancée?"

To her surprise, Ian shook his head vehemently, his expression grim. "No comment gentlemen," he said. "If you'll excuse us, M-m-miss Craig and I have a previous engagement."

By virtue of his size and strength, he literally shielded Bella with his body and muscled his way out of the pack of hungry newsmen. Moments later the two of them were standing outside. It had started to rain, a light mist that was cool and welcome after the crush in the gallery.

The prize committee had provided transportation for after the event as well. All Ian had to do was give his name. In no time, they were escorted to a comfortable vehicle and whisked away.

In the dark of the backseat, he loosened his tie and sighed. "Well, that wasn't too terrible. Could have been worse."

Bella sat and stewed. At last, even a bumbling male noticed. "What's wrong, Margaret?" he drawled. "Pining for handsome Harry?"

"That's absurd. I don't understand you," she said crossly. "The whole point of me coming with you tonight was to create a smokescreen. What happened to the elaborate story that was supposed to protect you from ravenous females and get you kicked off the eligible bachelor list?"

Ian didn't respond at first. Did he think she was using this opportunity to trap him somehow? Humiliation curled in her belly. "Your virtue is safe, Ian, I swear. Tonight was it for me. No more playacting. I don't know why you passed up a perfect moment to document me as your pretend fiancée, and I haven't a clue what those reporters thought, but you definitely missed your chance."

Suddenly, her companion leaned forward and tapped on the glass. "Driver, please take us up to Arthur's Seat... as far as the road allows."

The car made a U-turn. Soon they were back at the very spot where they had enjoyed a peaceful morning after last night's unpleasant confrontation. When the pavement ended, Ian helped Bella out, took her by the hand, and dismissed their only means of transportation.

The silence echoed as the sound of the car's engine faded into the distance. Ian held out his arm. "Take off your stockings. Give me your shoes. I'll carry you over the rough parts."

She could have protested. She should have backed away. Every moment she stayed with him found her sinking deeper into the quagmire.

Despite everything, she did as he commanded, as if she had neither an opinion nor a spine. Ian took the shoes and hosiery and tucked them into his jacket pockets. Fortunately, the rain had stopped but the air was thick with moisture.

They picked their way carefully to the top. Ian was as good as his word. Twice, he scooped her into his arms and carried her as if she weighed nothing at all. Any woman would have to be silly and shallow to be impressed by such a macho demonstration of brute strength. Apparently, Bella was both.

He set her down gently when they reached the summit. At this hour, they were alone.

She wrapped her arms around her waist. "Why did you bring me here?"

"I wanted to talk to you. I was afraid when we got back to the hotel we'd have to run the gauntlet again."

"So, talk." She shrugged as if whatever subject he might introduce was of no interest to her at all.

"Come here, woman." He scooped her up and sat down carefully, cuddling her in his lap. "I decided I couldn't call you my fiancée."

"I see."

To her embarrassment, she was unable to hide her wounded pride. Ian knew her far too well by now to be fooled. "It's not what you think, sweet Bella. The more I thought about my original plan, the sleazier it seemed. Promising to marry someone is a sacred thing. I decided I couldn't cheapen that vow by pretending. It wasn't right."

"I see." Apparently she only knew the two one-syllable words. This time, though, she wavered between relief and confusion. Since when did a cerebral scientist get to be so damned romantic and heartfelt?

As Ian held her closely against his chest, the tension gradually drained out of her body. His warmth and masculine scent surrounded her. The lights of Edinburgh were soft smudges in the misty air.

"Bella?" he said softly.

She nuzzled her head beneath his chin. "Yes?"

"I would very much like to make love to you tonight."

She respected the fact that he didn't dress it up with fancy words and flowery compliments. A man. A woman. No past. A doubtful future. Definitely a here and now.

"I'd like that, too," she said.

He tipped her back over his arm and kissed her. His lips were firm and coaxing as if recognizing her doubts. "God, you're beautiful," he said. He feathered his lips over her eyelids, her brow. "I don't know what to do about this…about *you*," he clarified gruffly. Palming one breast, he teased the nipple through two layers of silk. "It's eating me up inside."

"The feeling is mutual." Bella gasped as he slid a hand beneath her skirt. His long fingers were warm against her bare, chilled thigh. There was literally nowhere at all to do what they both wanted to do. Perched on a rocky promontory, they were exposed to the world…or they would have been if the world had been watching.

He kissed her again, this time harder, wilder. His tongue mated with hers, tasting of champagne and chocolate. "I want you more than I've ever wanted another woman. All I can think about is what it felt like to be inside you the other night. Tell me you want it, too. Or I'll stop. Right now. All you have to do is say no."

Raking her hands through his hair, she scraped his scalp with her fingernails. "Don't be an ass, Ian. Of course I want you. Can't you tell?"

Gently, he pressed a fingertip to the damp center of her lacy undies. "I suppose I can." His voice sounded like glass breaking. He trembled, although he was the one wearing a jacket while she was clad in nothing but a silk dress and cobweb dreams.

"Holder me tighter," she pleaded, "so I don't fly away." Her whole body shivered, not from cold, but with the intensity of the moment. Hunger clawed in her belly. "I'm on the pill," she muttered.

"Doesn't matter." His chuckle was rusty. "I brought a condom."

"Only one?"

* * *

Ian barked out a laugh when he could swear amusement was the furthest thing from his mind. His brain had turned to mush, his sex hogging all the blood supply. He plucked the pins from Bella's hair one at a time, winnowing his fingers through the thick, black silk as her sophisticated twist fell apart like some erotic commercial for shampoo.

The sharp edge of a boulder dug into his ass. He didn't care. His hands shook. His mouth was dry. "Are we really going to do this?"

Bella buried her face in his chest, her arms wrapped in a death grip around his waist. "I'm game if you are." She touched him carefully, testing the length and breadth of his desire through his pants. When he gasped and cursed helplessly, she lowered his zipper and took him in her hand.

Dizziness and lust dragged him under. "Stand up, Bella."

She did as he asked and shimmied her narrow skirt up her thighs until he could see the edge of her black thong. No wonder her perfect ass had been smooth under the black silk.

Recklessly, he took the tiny piece elastic at her hipbone and ripped it, tossing the remnant of silk and satin aside. The rush of raw satisfaction he got from that one quick move should have scared him. When Bella laughed low and wicked, he lost his mind.

She stood there like a siren on the rocks, coaxing him to his doom. Fumbling clumsily, he found the condom, opened it, and rolled it on. "Wait," he groaned, half blind from the dark haze of hunger.

Taking her by the hips, he pulled her close, helping her straddle his lap. "Hurry," she cried. "Before we get arrested."

"No hurrying," he said bluntly. "Not this time." With Bella standing and him sitting, he touched her gently, stroking the spot that made her sigh raggedly and put her hands on his shoulder.

She shuddered as he concentrated on making her whisper his name in supplication. That sound was about the sweetest thing he'd ever heard... and the most incendiary. Bella was close. He knew it. Curling an arm around her waist, he pressed his forehead to her ribcage. With his free hand, he continued his quest. One last teasing brush of his fingertip and she came with a choked cry.

He held her close as the ripples of release left her sated and weak. "Now, Bella," he said surging upward until he was buried inside her. "Now."

* * *

Afterward, Ian found himself embarrassingly weak and curiously absent from his body. Somewhere in the midst of their frenzy Bella had managed to twine her legs behind his back. Their bodies were still joined, damp with sweat that cooled rapidly in the night air.

"You're half naked," he muttered.

She nipped the side of his neck with sharp teeth. "Are you complaining, my genius lover?"

"Hell, no. I think I'd better get you back to civilization, though. You're shivering."

"I never get sick," she said blithely. "Sex outdoors is fun. I'm ticking off all sorts of firsts on this trip."

Something about her description bothered him, but he couldn't summon enough brain cells to understand why.

When Bella wiggled her way off his lap and stood, he held her hand as she straightened her dress. He'd likely ruined his tux pants. He got up as well and stifled a groan. After dealing with the condom and zipping his trousers, he rubbed his butt ruefully with both hands. "I think I may have a permanent sex injury," he complained. "Next time let's try for a flatter surface."

"This mountaintop thing was *your* idea," Bella pointed out.

"True." He stared down at her bare feet. What had he been thinking? "I'll have to piggyback you," he said. "It's getting too cold out here for you to walk, and your fancy shoes will be dangerous until we get down the flatter part of the trail."

"Oh, no," she said, her tone brooking no opposition. "Those rock steps are steep and wet. If one of us falls, no sense in both of us going down."

In the end, their descent was slow, but accident free. When they reached the spot where the car had dropped them off, Bella put her heels back on. She left the stockings in his pocket. He hadn't a clue if she was miserable or not, but she never complained.

He tried to call a cab, but none were available at the moment.

"I can walk," Bella said firmly. "These shoes are more comfortable than they look."

They set off toward the hotel holding hands. He would have given just about anything to know what she was thinking. On paper, he was a genius, but when it came to the female brain, he was as clueless as the next fellow.

Now that the ceremony at the palace was over, another disconcerting reality loomed. It was possible that this feeling in his gut was infinitely more than passing interest in a pretty woman.

He had *feelings* for Bella. Real, complicated human emotions. That much he understood. What was less clear were the options for pursuing a connection that was tenuous at best.

Bella enjoyed his company. She even decoded his sense of humor and appeared to "get" him. Though he spent far too many hours alone in his ordinary workaday life, Bella had unwittingly taught him to enjoy the presence of another human being when he was working.

But did he love her? His libido shied away from the topic, determined to keep tonight's agenda on a carnal level. Bella wasn't going anywhere. He had time to figure this out.

At the hotel they were able to walk through the front door without incident. The messy weather and the late hour had discouraged the gutter press. Although the lobby was empty, the front desk clerk raised an eye at their appearance. Bella's hair was a nimbus around her head. Ian's pants were wrinkled, and his shoes were caked in mud where he had inadvertently stumbled off the path.

Side by side, they walked up the narrow stairs. Bella stopped at her room and smiled. "Good night, Ian."

"Bella," he said urgently. Backing her against the door he kissed her roughly, his hands on her shoulders. "I don't want to say good night."

Big blue eyes searched his face. "I'm a mess. We both are. Shouldn't we go on to bed?"

"To bed? Hell, yes." He cupped her cheeks in his hands. "I want to sleep with you, lass. After I make love to you again. Am I making too many assumptions? What do *you* want, lovely girl?"

If he could have read the secrets in her eyes, his feet might have found solid ground. As it was, he was adrift and sinking. He knew what he wanted in the next ten seconds, but he couldn't see past the end of the hall, much less into a future that included Bella Craig.

She sighed...a long, drawn out sound that told him she was as conflicted as he was. "Okay, Ian. My room. Only after we've both had half an hour to clean up. Deal?"

He nodded. "Deal."

* * *

Bella stripped off her beautiful new dress and tossed it on a chair. Only then did she remember she was naked from the waist down. She groaned aloud. What kind of woman leaves her underpants on top of Arthur's Seat in the middle of Edinburgh?

In the bathroom, she avoided the mirror. She knew her hair was out of control, and on top of that, she didn't really want to face the doubt she would see in her own eyes. Ian had practically come right out and said he wasn't interested in anything more than meaningless sex. All that talk about Prince Harry choosing to play the field, and Ian not wanting to call Bella his fiancée even as a ruse.

The man was a confirmed bachelor.

Despite the many reasons she should cut and run, Bella took a shower, dried her hair, and put on the sexiest PJs she had packed. The teal T-shirt said *Bookworms Rock.* It was large and sloppy, and it covered her to mid-thigh, because she had purposely bought it two sizes too large.

Ian was prompt. His quiet knock came exactly thirty-one minutes after he had disappeared into his own room. When she opened the door, he gave her a lopsided smile that curled her toes and tightened other spots. "I was hoping you hadn't changed your mind."

She dragged him inside, took a quick peek out into the hall to make sure nobody was watching, and locked the door. "I haven't," she said. "You look nice."

His feet were bare, his hair damp from his shower. He had tugged on jeans and a black cotton crewneck sweater.

Earlier tonight, the man in the tux had carried himself with sophistication and confidence. This Scotsman looked out-of-control, his body vibrating with tension and barely leashed hunger.

Ian didn't wait for an invitation. He took the hem of her T-shirt and raised it, tugging it off over her head. His quick, sharp inhaled breath told her he approved the fact that she was bare underneath. "I hope you weren't planning on sleeping," he muttered, gliding his hands over her breasts and thumbing the tips.

She shook her head. "I can sleep when I'm dead." His sweater came off as easily as her top. She put her hands, palms flat, on his hair-dusted chest. His skin was hot. She almost expected her fingertips to sizzle. For a nerd-genius he was in incredibly good shape.

Ian lifted her and backed her against the door. "Tell me what you want, Bella."

She smiled at him hazily, feeling everything morph into slow motion. "I want it all."

Chapter Eighteen

Bella didn't have a headache this time when the sun peeked in. On the other hand, finding herself clearheaded and in possession of vivid memories from the night before was almost as devastating.

She and Ian had barely slept, and then only in snatches. The man was a machine. Every time she fell asleep, she awoke to find his hands caressing her as if he had to learn every peak and valley of her body. In the midst of wild lovemaking, he murmured words of Gaelic to her all night long. Too bashful to ask for a translation, Bella had let the musical language sink into her soul.

At the moment, a large male arm pinned her to the bed. When she wiggled experimentally, the arm tightened, but the Scotsman didn't open his eyes. No matter. Maybe they could spend the whole day in bed.

Reaching for her phone, she peered bleary-eyed at the screen and squawked in dismay. "Get up, Ian. We have to check out in twenty minutes." She eluded his grasp, jumped out of bed, and started throwing things in her suitcase.

He raised up on his elbows and frowned. "Dinna fash yerself, lass. We'll call downstairs and tell them we want to stay another night."

"We can't do that, you big crazy man," she said, trying not to be distracted by his naked magnificence. "I already asked yesterday to extend our stay so we could play tourist, and they said they have a large tour group arriving this afternoon. The whole hotel is booked."

Ian groaned and muttered something under his breath. "I forgot," he said. He closed his eyes and squinted as she threw open the drapes. "Lord help me, you're a cruel woman."

"Up, Larrimore. Now."

It was all she could do not to swoon like a Victorian maiden when he tossed the sheet aside and rolled to his feet, buck naked. How in the world had she ended up in bed with this man? She was more accustomed to skinny, pasty-complexioned doctoral students. Males she could understand and control.

While she fretted and dressed, Ian took his time. The more she hurried him, the slower he moved. Finally, she put her hands on her hips and pointed at the door. "Go to your room."

"Kinky schoolmarm. I like it." He waggled his eyebrows.

She flushed. "Quit driving me nuts, would you?"

"All we have to do is move to another hotel," he said mildly.

It was tempting. So. Very. Tempting. But good sense prevailed. "Too much trouble. Besides, I want to go home and see my brother and McKenzie."

* * *

An hour later, they were on the motorway headed north. Neither of them had eaten much breakfast. Bella's stomach was queasy. Ian had gone incommunicado, his mood borderline surly.

Unlike the trip down to Edinburgh, today there were no leisurely stops to exclaim over the view or to explore ruined churches. The man behind the wheel drove steadily at five kilometers over the speed limit. He barely stopped for lunch, and even that was a quick sandwich at a small grocery store with an old-fashioned lunch counter.

At three o'clock, they were still an hour and a half away from Portree. Without warning, Ian steered the car onto the side of the road, turned off the engine, and rotated his neck. "I have to sleep for a few minutes," he said. "Do you want to drive?"

She shuddered. "On the wrong side of the road? Not even a little bit. We can both nap."

He nodded curtly and lowered the windows. The afternoon breeze was pleasant. He reclined his seat and was unconscious in seconds.

Bella was equally exhausted, but she couldn't stop thinking about the night before. The marathon sex had been incredible, but her fascination with Ian went far beyond that. He challenged her…made her laugh. It was a guilty pleasure to watch him while he slept. Thick eyelashes shielded the sharp intelligence in his wicked gaze. He hadn't bothered to shave in their mad dash to leave the hotel. His sculpted chin carried the shadow of stubble that made him both wildly attractive and less domesticated.

She closed her eyes and leaned back in her seat, but she was jumpy and unsettled. Quietly, she retrieved her phone from her purse and began to scroll through e-mails. Some of them were completely disconnected from her present circumstances. Her life back in North Carolina seemed like a fondly remembered dream.

Even sleep-deprived, she knew such an impression was dangerous. Portree wasn't *her* life; it was Finley's. Visiting her brother was all well and good, but she had to make her own choices, follow her own path.

Suddenly, her throat tightened as she read the subject line of a very official-looking e-mail from the university. She clicked on the box and read the lengthy communication. When she was done, she exited the app and stared out the windshield, her hands cold and her brain awhirl with scattered thoughts.

It had seemed as if she had plenty of time to decide what to do about Ian Larrimore. Apparently, not as long as she thought.

* * *

They arrived back in Portree hungry and tired and more than ready for the delicious meal McKenzie and Finley had put together to welcome them home. As Ian watched, Bella threw herself into her brother's arms. "I've missed you," she cried, kissing his cheek. Then she turned to her new sister-in-law with a shy smile. "I'm especially happy to see you. I thought you might have come to your senses and abandoned ship by now."

McKenzie, as blond and beautiful as Bella was dark-headed and lovely, beamed and rested her cheek against her husband's shoulder. "He's a handful, but I'll keep him. No one else would put up with his nonsense. I suppose I'm in for the duration."

Finley kissed his wife soundly, ignoring their audience. "Damned straight," he said with the trace of a southern accent Ian remembered. "So how was Edinburgh? How was the queen? We want to hear all about it."

McKenzie nodded. "And after that, I'll bore you with five hundred photos of the Greek Isles."

"Sounds good to me," Ian said. Bella had yet to make eye contact with him since they walked through the front door, though he didn't know why. Perhaps he hadn't been the best traveling companion on the way back today, but Lord, his head had ached. Nothing a meal and a good night's sleep wouldn't fix.

Over crisp chilled wine and sautéed veal medallions, the four adults settled into a comfortable conversation. Finley was the common denominator in the group. Brother. Husband. Friend. The other three had more ground to cover.

Ian found himself laughing often and relaxing more than he expected. McKenzie was whip smart and had a sense of humor that matched the rest of the group. Finley had mellowed in the year since Ian had last seen him. Though the two men talked about motorcycles in passing, the evening was more about the things all four had in common than the differences that separated them.

By the end of the night, Ian was feeling damn good about life in general. He was a lucky man.

His euphoria lasted right up until the moment Bella sked her brother a pointed question.

"Have you already brought my mattress down to your office, Finley?" she asked, her expression guileless. "As soon as we finish cleaning up dinner, I'm off to bed. I'm exhausted."

"It's all ready for you, Sis. McKenzie made sure of that."

Ian had to pick his chin up off the floor. And then he realized what was going on. Clearly, Bella didn't want Finley to know she and Ian had become intimate. Made sense. After everybody was asleep, she would join Ian in the guest room. At least that was his assumption.

While Finley and McKenzie cleared the table, Ian pulled Bella aside to make sure. "Are we keeping our private life private?" he asked with a grin.

She couldn't quite meet his eyes. "I'd rather be low key about you and me," she said. "And besides, both of us could use a good night's sleep."

Ian knew a brush-off when he heard one. His temper simmered. "You *could* sleep with me. After Finley and McKenzie go to bed. We're all grown adults. I'm sure Finley knows his baby sister has needs."

Bella's eyes flashed. "Don't be crude, Ian."

He frowned. "I wasn't. All I'm saying is that your brother doesn't have the right to make judgments about your personal life."

Finley and McKenzie returned at exactly the wrong moment. The tension in the room was palpable.

McKenzie's gaze darted from Bella to Ian and back again. "Everything okay in here?"

Bella's smile was weary but seemed genuine. "I was just telling Ian how glad I am to have a new sister."

* * *

Bella escaped to her temporary bedroom without having to be alone with Ian again. She knew he was upset, but she was upset too. Did she want to spend the night in the guest room with him? Of course she did. Life would be way simpler if all she had to think about was sex. She was in love with a man who had more layers than an onion. She honestly had no idea if he cared about her at all.

Finley had added a downstairs bathroom adjacent to his office several years ago, so she had privacy to get ready for bed. She finished brushing her teeth and had just climbed under the covers with a book when her brother knocked on the door.

"Come in," she said.

Finley ducked under the doorway. Parts of his quirky house seemed to have been designed for elves or dwarves. "You sure you're okay sleeping on the floor?" he asked with a small frown.

"I'm fine. Quit worrying."

Finley pulled out the desk chair and sat down, his arms folded over his chest. "I'll never stop worrying about you, Bella. You saved my life more than once, and I can never make up for leaving you to handle Dad all those years."

She sat up pretzel style and pulled her hair into a side ponytail. "You did what you had to do. I never blamed you, not really."

"So what's the deal with you and Ian?"

"It's complicated."

"Seriously? You're going to lie to your own brother?"

"I'm not lying," she said crossly. "It *is* complicated. I like him, and—" She grimaced, not sure how to put the situation into words her brother would understand. Heck, Bella didn't really understand it.

"You've slept with him, haven't you?" Finley looked more troubled than judgmental.

"Since when do we compare notes about our sex lives?"

"Mine is an open book." He said it with the smug satisfaction of a man who was getting laid on a regular basis.

"Fine. Yes. I slept with Ian. Is that a crime?"

Finley leaned forward, his elbows resting on his knees. His troubled expression unsettled her. "I was serious when Finley first arrived and I told you I wasn't matchmaking. He's a great guy. I like him a lot. The thing is, though…" Now it was Finley's turn to search for words.

"What? He's married? He's a convicted felon? You might as well tell me the worst."

Finley shrugged, his gaze unhappy. "He's a genius, no question…and a stand-up guy. But he's not emotionally available."

Bella narrowed her eyes. "Since when does my biker brother throw around phrases like *emotionally available*?"

"McKenzie has reformed me." His grin was rueful. "Honestly, Bella, I don't want you to get hurt. You have this huge heart and a capacity for emotional depth that's pretty damn amazing considering that Dad and I were your main role models growing up. I don't think you know how to protect yourself, because you believe people are basically kind and decent."

"You're saying Ian is *not* kind and decent? For a man who claims to be his friend, that's low."

"I'm trying to tell you he's unpredictable. Those same brain cells of his that come up with incredible new ideas are focused somewhere other than the people around him. You deserve a man who puts you first."

She blinked, stunned to hear her brother articulate the very thing she had told herself not so long ago. Was it wrong to want that from Ian when he had so much to offer the world at large?

"I'll be careful," she said, climbing off the mattress and kneeling beside Finley to rest her head against his knee. Her brother stroked her hair, the same way he had done when she was nine years old and woke up from a nightmare. In many ways, he had been more like a father than a brother to her.

Finley sighed. "You know, Bella, you can stay with us as long as you want. McKenzie and I have discussed it. We enjoy having you around. The house is plenty big. Ian probably won't be here much longer."

The truth in that statement depressed her. "Thank you," she said. "I'd like to linger for another week or ten days. Even though I'll be headed home soon, maybe I can come back for Christmas."

"Or who knows, McKenzie and I may be in Atlanta. We'll keep our options open."

When a yawn caught her by surprise, Finley took the hint. "Good night, kiddo. Get some sleep. Everything will look better in the morning."

* * *

After resting barely at all the night before in Edinburgh, Bella was out cold in no time. She slept hard and deep. Snatches of dreams lurked in her memory when she awoke the next morning, but she wasn't able to piece together a single coherent scene. Even so, the feeling she had was one of distress.

Shaking off the unknown wisps of mental struggles, she showered and dressed. The other three were already seated around the kitchen table when she appeared.

Finley held out her favorite mug. "Coffee, Sis?"

She nodded. "Oh, yeah."

Ian had showered and shaved and was wearing his usual khakis and a navy cotton shirt. His expression was guarded, but she might have been the only one who noticed.

"I have some news," she said. She'd spent hours mulling it over. Now seemed as good a time as any to spill the beans.

McKenzie lifted an eyebrow. "Don't keep us in suspense."

"I had an e-mail from my faculty advisor yesterday. Two professors in the history department have left unexpectedly for health reasons. The university has offered me a teaching position. It's a non-tenured spot, but it would cover the cost of my remaining dissertation fees and give me income while I do the work. The letter was very flattering."

Finley smiled broadly. "That's great. They know talent when they see it."

"You might be a tad prejudiced," Bella said wryly. She shot Ian a sideways glance. "I have to give them an answer very soon. It seems like the sensible thing to do."

Ian sat stone-faced. "What about your novel?" he asked abruptly. All eyes were on him suddenly.

"Novel?" Finley frowned in confusion.

Bella flushed. "It's only something I mentioned to Ian in passing. A bucket list item. Right now I need to finish my dissertation and move on with my life. I've been puttering around too long."

"Excuse me, will you? I have some calls I need to make." Ian stood up abruptly, almost overturning his chair, and disappeared before his breakfast companions could do more than blink.

"What did you do to piss him off?" Finley asked, correctly reading the situation.

"I have no idea," she lied. "I may have given him the impression I wasn't satisfied with my life plan, but I was wrong. It makes perfect sense to finish the dissertation now that I'm this close. Even if I don't want to teach right away, I'll have the degree to fall back on."

"Well of course it does," Finley said, carrying his plate to the sink. "You'd be a fool to quit now after all your hard work."

Bella finished her coffee and brooded. The piece of toast she'd consumed sat like lead in her stomach. "It's a beautiful day," she said. "I think I'll head out and explore the island for a while."

McKenzie smiled. "You want some company, or would you rather be alone? Finley's probably going to be in the shop all day."

"I have some thinking to do. I promise not to go anywhere dangerous. Thanks, anyway. I'll take you up on your offer next time."

Her main goal was to escape before Ian came back downstairs.

Grabbing the keys to the car, she headed out, then drove aimlessly as the hours crept by. By now, she knew her way around really well. Skye felt comfortable, though still exotic and inspiring.

One thing became crystal clear as she pondered the invitation from the university. It was impossible to say yes to *that* commitment until she clarified where she stood with Ian…or if his response to her was anything more than physical at all.

Why couldn't she simply tell him the truth? Say that she loved him? Ask if he had any feelings for her? It was the only way to get closure before her return to the States. If by some miracle he reciprocated, they could move forward with melding their two very different lives.

If Ian didn't love her, the answer was equally simple. She would hop a plane and go back to North Carolina.

Chapter Nineteen

Having a solid plan helped lighten Bella's mood. If the worst happened and Ian had to "let her down gently" as they said in the *Cosmo* advice columns, she was a big girl. She could handle it.

But life threw her a curve she hadn't expected. When she got back to Finley's house, Ian was gone.

"What do you mean, he's gone?" she demanded, trying not to lose it completely.

The expression in her brother's eyes was a mixture of sympathy and frustration. "I'm saying he packed up his things after breakfast, gave me some dumb-ass excuse about being needed back at work, and lit out of here like he stepped on a rocket."

"Did you point out it might be polite of him to linger and tell me good-bye himself?"

"Of course I did," Finley shouted. "The man cleaned out his room and drove away. I don't know what else to tell you."

Bella burst into tears, big ugly sobs that burned her chest and left her embarrassed and miserable.

McKenzie glared at her new husband. "Go build a motorcycle or something. This is a problem for women to deal with. You're making things worse."

Finley didn't need a second invitation. He disappeared faster than snow in the desert.

"I'm sorry," Bella blubbered, wiping her face with both hands. "You're on your honeymoon. I'm ruining everything."

McKenzie took her hand and led her to the loveseat. "Don't be so dramatic," she said calmly. "Nothing is ruined, and to be honest, I think you should be excited that Ian left so abruptly."

Bella gaped. "What do you mean?"

"I mean that your big, macho scientist heard you talk about going home and he freaked out."

"I don't think that's what happened."

"I was there. I saw his face. Do you have another explanation?"

"He's not really hiding out from the press anymore. I think he tolerates it now. The award ceremony with the queen is over. He probably really did need to get back to work."

"Without saying good-bye to you?"

"He wasn't sure how long I would be gone today."

"Fine." McKenzie sighed. "I'll tell you, though, the man is not indifferent to you."

Bella would have laughed if she hadn't been so distraught. The distance between *not indifferent* and *love* was as wide as the ocean that would soon separate her from Ian. "I don't know what to do," she whispered, her throat raw from crying.

McKenzie wrapped both arms around Bella and held on tight. "You said you have ten days before you need to go back to the real world. Use that time to step out in faith and decide what it is you really want."

* * *

Ian shouldn't have been driving. Though he was stone cold sober, his much-touted brain was useless. *Bella was leaving him.* The gaping hole in his chest made it hard to breathe. He'd never been an impulsive man. His method of attack when it came to problems was to lay out the parameters, study the variables, and predict various outcomes based on the data in hand.

The scientific method was a joke when it came to understanding women.

When he set out from Portree, he'd intended to drive straight through to London. Instead, he found himself taking the turnoff toward Glasgow. Four hours later, he pulled into a carpark alongside a beige, institutional building. The grounds were nicely tended, but nothing could disguise the sadness inside those walls. He gipped the steering wheel until his knuckles turned white.

What was the point of stopping by? She wouldn't know who he was. She hadn't recognized him for a long time. Still, he made the trip on her birthday and at Christmas. Today was neither.

His father, God love his crotchety, closed-off self, dutifully came twice a month. To this day, Ian didn't really understand why. This woman had betrayed her wedding vows, abandoned her husband and young son, and ruined the reputation of a man to whom she had pledged her eternal devotion.

Even more inexplicable than Ian's father's regular visits was the fact that the senior Mr. Larrimore had married his wife a second time when she became ill and needed health insurance. Ian had never understood and likely never would.

The urge to flee was strong, but now that he had driven this far, it seemed crazy to walk away. Instead, he got out of the car, trudged up the shallow front steps, waited to be buzzed in by security, and signed the visitor register in the lobby.

His mother's room was on the third floor. She had a private suite with a view that looked out over the gardens in the back.

The door was ajar. Ian knocked quietly and entered.

Often he found his mother in bed dozing. Sometimes her attention would be fixed raptly on the TV set mounted high on the wall. Today, she sat in a comfy armchair by the window. Though her hearing was perfectly normal, she gave no sign that she recognized his approach.

He studied her in that moment, trying to remember a day when he had been part of a happy family of three. The image wouldn't come into focus. All he could claim were wispy recollections—the scent of her perfume, the way she laughed, the warmth of the kitchen when she was cooking.

"Mother," he said. "It's me. Ian. I've stopped by to say hello."

Still she stared out the window. Sighing inwardly, he sat down in the second chair. Now their knees practically bumped. Surely she knew he was there.

"Mother..." He tried again.

At last her head swiveled in his direction. Her once beautiful auburn hair was white, pulled back by some caretaker into a bun on the back of her head. Though years ago her skin had been soft and pale, betraying her Irish heritage, now her face and hands were wrinkled and sallow.

She gazed at him, her pale blue eyes vacant. "Did ye bring the ice cream, boy? I told them I wanted vanilla."

He floundered, never accustomed to the random zigs and zags of her conversation. "It will be here soon," he said, knowing she would soon forget whatever it was that prompted the request. "Do you know who I am?" He'd given up asking that question years ago, yet still he grasped at a connection that wasn't there.

Her blue-tinged lips trembled. Without responding, she ignored him and returned her attention to the world outside the window. It was her way. Whenever something upset her, she vanished inside her head.

They sat there in silence for an hour. Ian had come looking for something, though he couldn't have said for what or why. Nothing about his life had ever been normal...whatever the hell normal was. Even so, he'd found a measure of peace in his studies and his work.

Most parents hoped their children would inherit the best of both gene pools. Ian had always been terrified his DNA included the worst. Though he wasn't a substance abuser, some would say he was addicted to his research and his own company. As for the Y chromosome, Ian had a small circle of friends, but was he really anymore sociable than his taciturn, close-mouthed dad?

He kept vigil with his mother for an hour. The mix of emotions in his gut was the same as always. Guilt. Pity. Distress.

It hurt to see this frail, frightened woman a prisoner in her own fragile, damaged brain.

Finally, he forced himself mentally to let her go. It was the same every time...almost like a death. He stood up slowly, so as not to startle her. Picking up his cell phone from the bed where he had laid it, he glanced down to see if he had any messages. There were none.

Stepping away from the window, he tried to end the visit on a positive note. "Your flowers are beautiful." The small crystal vase sat on the table beside her bed.

At last, she looked at him again. The querulous frown was the most expression he had seen on her face today. "Your father brought them. I told him I hate carnations, but he never listens to me...."

One moment of lucidity, and then it was gone. Ian wanted to laugh and cry at the same time. For a split second his poor addled mother connected the dots correctly, but only to criticize her disappointing spouse.

He bent and kissed the top of her head. "I have to go now, Mama. It's a long way back to London." Six hours. Not so far at all. But he'd had all he could bear of this soul-crushing family reunion.

Her hands twisted in her lap, picking at a fold in her flowered cotton dress. "Have you seen the puppy?" she asked. "I don't want him making a mess on the stairs like he did last night."

"I'll find him and take him out," Ian said, his heart flinching inwardly. "Good-bye, Mama."

* * *

Four months later…

Bella hurried up three flights of steps in the echoing stairwell and unlocked the oak door to her tiny, old-fashioned office. She'd been back on campus for an entire semester, and it was as if she had never left. Her time in Scotland seemed like a dream. Mostly. There were nights when she still cried herself to sleep, but that was understandable. Right?

After accepting the job offer from the university and doing her best to enjoy her last ten days in Scotland, she had flown home right on schedule. Diving into work helped take her mind off her broken heart. She was in love with Ian, but he didn't love her back. She was neither the first nor the last woman to find herself in such a situation.

Though she checked the tabloids for news of him, as she had predicted, other stories now dominated the news cycle. It was impossible to keep up with her Scottish bachelor, even secondhand.

Moving on with her life was the hardest thing she had ever done. For the first month, she had checked her e-mail obsessively, convinced Ian would write a note and say he wanted her to return to Scotland. Gradually, the truth became inescapable.

Ian didn't want her. The one saving grace was that she never had a chance to tell him she loved him. He had left Finley's house so abruptly the words she had finally decided to say were left unsaid. It was for the best.

The only exception to his absolute radio silence was the arrival of a small package with her name on it and a Scottish postmark. Although there was no note, she assumed it had to be from him, particularly when she saw was what inside. She stared at the contents in shock. The navy leather box held a necklace and matching earrings, the ones she had seen in a shop window on the Royal Mile. The amber pendant seemed to glow. The gold chain and the gold trim on the earrings was delicate and feminine.

It hurt to look at them.

Stoically, she had shut the box and stuffed it on the back of a high shelf in her closet where she wouldn't have to look at it. Her tears were all used up. Now, all she felt was a deep, aching regret.

She abandoned the memories and dragged her attention back to the task at hand, refusing to go forward into the holidays with a maudlin mood. As she entered final semester grades in her laptop for the freshmen who had taken her European History course, she glanced out the window now and again. Snow fell in blustery gusts. Soon it would begin piling up. The forecasters predicted six inches by morning. Bella was prepared.

She had a fridge full of food and was looking forward to a weekend of binge watching television and wrapping Christmas presents. In a week, she would be joining Finley and McKenzie in Atlanta for the holidays. Finley and his bride had made the decision to split the year between their respective homes. April through September in Portree, the fall and winter months in Georgia.

It felt odd but nice to have nothing looming over her head. Her dissertation was finished. She had defended it with flying colors. Though she'd chosen not to participate in tomorrow's mid-year graduation ceremony, she was now officially *Dr.* Craig.

Oddly, that didn't give her the boost of excitement it once had. The goal seemed anticlimactic. Even so, come mid-January, she would be teaching a full load of classes. The head of the department had hinted strongly that with one of the two ill faculty members choosing to retire, the future looked bright for Bella's career aspirations.

She wasn't at all sure how she felt about that prospect. Her novel, barely begun, still beckoned. Perhaps like her relationship with Ian, though, it was no more than an unlikely pipedream.

At last—her immediate responsibilities completed—she closed her laptop and decided it was time to head home. She didn't want to be caught in the worst of the snowfall. She put the out-of-office message on her phone and was seconds away from walking out when a firm knock broke the silence.

Sighing, she arranged her face in a pleasant expression and called out in a cheerful voice. "Come in."

When the door swung open slowly and she saw who it was, her heart sank to the floor, shot to the ceiling, and fell again in dizzying succession. She cleared her throat. "Hello, Ian. What brings you here?"

* * *

Ian saw in an instant that Bella was perfectly at home in her surroundings. Much the same way he flourished in a lab, Bella reveled in academia. The ivy-covered buildings, the beautiful quad turning white with snow, the gentle, steady pace of learning and growth.

He faltered only for a moment. "Hello, Bella," he said quietly. "I checked your schedule online. I was hoping you were finished for the day and might be free to join me for dinner. I'd like to talk." When she opened her mouth to protest, he held up a hand. "You don't have to say a word. Honestly. But I have some things I need to get off my chest."

Her gaze was guarded, even tense. "Is it really so important, Ian? You and I have been apart twice as long as we actually knew each other, more than that actually."

She was right. In some ways he felt like he had lived a lifetime since he walked out of Finley's house. In other aspects, the wound was raw.

"Please," he said. "I owe you an apology. I'd like a chance to explain."

"It's not necessary."

"It is to me." For several long agonizing heartbeats he thought she was going to kick him out. It wouldn't have mattered. He had no plans to go anywhere else until he settled things with Bella.

"Okay." She surrendered gracefully, though her face gave nothing away in regard to her true emotions.

"Thank you," he said. Was she at all glad to see him, or had he killed whatever affection existed between them?

"Let me get my coat," she said, reaching for a hook on the back of the door. "I don't know what you had in mind for dinner, but in case you aren't aware, the forecast is nasty."

"Yes," he said, helping her into her camel-colored wool jacket. "I rented a Range Rover to be on the safe side."

"That'll work."

At last she gave him a faint smile. He felt as if he had won the lottery or climbed a challenging mountain peak. Waiting patiently while she gathered her things for the long holiday, he then took most of it from her arms and stepped into the hall as she locked the door.

He wanted to dump everything on the floor, shove her up against the wall, and kiss her. He had given up that right, though, when he walked out of Finley's house without saying good-bye. Had he ruined things beyond repair?

When they made it outside, he wanted to wrap an arm around her and shelter her from the icy wind. Her body language warned him to keep his distance. Bella was proud and resourceful and strong. She didn't need a man to play out some macho fantasy.

He had already scoped out the route to the restaurant. After putting Bella's things in the back of the Rover, they both climbed in, and Ian shut the doors. Now they were enclosed in a bubble of intimacy.

Doggedly, he started the engine and backed out. This afternoon was turning out to be much more difficult than he had anticipated.

"Are you warm enough?" he asked.

"Yes."

"Do you want music or no music? Feel free to pick a station."

She was probably as eager as he was to fill the heavy silence. The touch screen on the dashboard yielded a dozen choices. When Bella chose one, the sound of a classic Christmas tune filled the air with cheer. *Oh, there's no place like home for the holidays…*

That had never been the case at his house. From what he had heard of Finley and Bella's childhood and adolescence, they had not experienced such simple holiday magic either.

Fortunately for his plans, the restaurant he had chosen was still open, but much of the clientele had stayed away. Which meant that the maître d' was able to give them the best seat in the house, a private cozy corner booth with a window that framed the postcard scene outside.

"This is lovely," Bella said, looking around with interest. "I've never eaten here."

He'd deliberately picked the kind of restaurant most people reserved for special occasions. He wanted the ambiance and the food to underscore his efforts. So far, it was working. Though Bella was far from relaxed, she at least seemed more open than she had when he first showed up in her office.

After the sommelier stopped by the table to offer wine, their waiter handed over menus and rattled off the evening's specials. "I recommend the prime rib, the asparagus, and the pumpkin pie," he said. "All are excellent."

Ian lost his nerve when Bella spent an inordinate amount of time studying the entrée selections. He was almost certain she was trying to ignore him. That wasn't going to happen if he had anything to say about it.

He had treated her badly. There was no other way to describe it, but it was Christmas, damn it, and he would beg for a chance to be heard if necessary. "Is it so difficult to even look me in the eye?" he asked, his pride in ruins. "God knows, Bella, I deserve your contempt, but if you can find it in your heart to listen with an open mind, I'd like you to understand why I ran."

* * *

Bella alternated between feeling faint and nauseated. She had no idea why Ian was here. It would be emotional suicide to assume a happy ending. He could be ready to say anything at all.

Still, hope swelled in her chest.

The man looked terrible, to be honest. He had lost at least fifteen pounds, maybe more given his height. His expression was sober. In his eyes she saw a reflection of the suffering she had endured.

"I'm sorry," she said, meeting his gaze directly for the first time. "I wasn't expecting you to show up on my doorstep. It rattled me."

"I get that. I didn't mean to make it some huge surprise, but when I thought about texting or calling or e-mailing you, I was afraid it would give you too many options to get rid of me."

"Wouldn't that be the smart thing to do on my part?" she asked wryly.

He flushed. "I don't want to hurt you at all, yet even as I say that, it seems presumptuous to assume I could."

Bella eyed him cautiously. If there was ever a time for honesty, it was now. "You could," she said bluntly. "You did."

Chapter Twenty

As soon as she uttered the words, she wanted to snatch them back. Being vulnerable and open sucked.

Ian winced. "I am so very sorry, Bella."

"Why did you do it?" she asked steadily. "Why did you leave without saying good-bye?" It was a question she had wrestled with during weeks of sleepless nights.

He took a sip of his wine, almost casually, but the fingers of his left hand drummed restlessly on the tablecloth. "That morning at breakfast when you said the university had offered you a job, it stunned me. I couldn't believe you hadn't told me, but then I realized it was something you would share with family first. Even so, what you said sent me into a tailspin."

"Why, Ian?"

"I had started having feelings for you, but I was so damn confused about what I wanted. I was terrified that I had inherited the worst from both of my parents…my mother's instability and my father's inability to connect with people he loved."

"You've never struck me as unstable. Far from it."

He grimaced. "I notice that you didn't discount the second part."

"Well," she said, trying to be transparent about her feelings, "I honestly didn't know how to read you. I was sure you enjoyed the sex, but men are wired that way. I hadn't a clue if you thought of me as anything other than a relatively new friend with benefits."

Reaching across the table, he took her right hand in both of his, and rubbed the back of it with two thumbs. "I didn't know what to think, Arabella Margaret. It was like my life had been the *Wizard of Oz* in black and white, and then you came, and my world burst into color."

"Oh, Ian." No one had ever said such a thing to her. She could see in his eyes that he meant it. "I have something to tell you, too," she said. "The day you left—while I was out exploring—I had made the decision to tell you I was in love with you. I had no clue what would happen after that, but I held out hope that you would be glad to hear it."

He released her hand and sat back in his chair, his expression tormented. "Good God, Bella. I don't know what to say."

She shrugged. "It's just as well I hadn't already said it. That way I could go home and pretend you and I never happened."

"I loved you, too," he said slowly. "But I didn't *know* I loved you. Do you even believe me when I say that?"

Loved. Past tense. That hurt. "Of course I believe you. What I don't get is why you had to leave. I wasn't trying to squeeze a commitment out of you. Surely you knew that."

"I never thought it for a minute. I was too busy running from reporters and trying to decide why the prospect of going back to my normal life in London was so unappealing. When you told us at breakfast that morning the university had offered you a job, I was shocked. I could hear in your voice that you planned to accept. I panicked."

"But why?"

"I had nothing to offer you. I might be smart, but I had no guarantee that I wouldn't be like my father and forget to pay attention to you."

"So you were afraid I would eventually run away and become a drug addict and spiral into self-destruction?"

The conversation halted when their food appeared. Bella had never felt less like eating, but she picked at her mashed potatoes.

Ian thanked the waiter and sent him on his way. His jaw squared like it did when he was displeased. "When you say it that way, it sounds ridiculous."

"If the shoe fits."

He chewed a bite of beef and swallowed it, his expression stormy. "I went to see my mother that day...the day I left Portree. I wanted to understand why my father still loved her, still cared for her when she had done nothing but hurt him his entire life."

"And did you discover the answer to your question?"

Ian gave her a small rueful smile. "Actually no. I didn't. Apparently love is something that can't be explained. It simply *is*. The notion doesn't make sense on a scientific level, which is why I struggled so hard to grasp it."

"Your father must have suffered a great deal." And his young son had been there to witness it year after year.

"I do believe he loved her and loves her still. At one time I thought things could have been different if only he had only been able to show her. Now, I'm not so sure. She was a deeply flawed woman with problems beyond our ken to help her."

"Ian..." She felt the few bites of potatoes she had eaten congeal into a lump in her stomach.

"What?"

"Did you really fly across an ocean to talk about your mother?"

His eyes glittered. "I think you know the answer to that question." He glanced at his prime cut of beef with displeasure. "Would you mind if we get out of here?"

"It's an expensive meal."

"I don't give a damn about how much it cost. I was wrong to bring you here. Please tell me you live close by. And that you'll let me come home with you to get in out of the cold."

Her heart fizzed. "I have pizza in the freezer."

"Good."

"But no guest room."

"I suppose that could be good or bad depending upon your perspective."

The little flutters that had started in her stomach filled her chest now. "My car is still at work."

"I'll take you wherever you need to go."

They rose in silence. Ian tossed a hundred-dollar bill on the table and anchored it with the candleholder.

The waiter rushed over aghast. "Is there a problem with the meal, madam? Sir?"

Bella smiled at him dreamily. "It was delicious, but we've decided it might be dangerous to linger any longer...the snow, you know."

"A takeout container," the employee offered desperately, clearly worried that his Yelp score was going to tumble.

Bella went up on tiptoe and gave the startled older man a kiss on the cheek. "Merry Christmas. The meal was fine...wonderful, even. We've just discovered somewhere we need to be."

* * *

Ian brought the Range Rover around to the front door of the restaurant, half afraid Bella might have disappeared in the short time he had been gone.

Clearly miracles really did happen at Christmas, because his beautiful, sometimes aggravating date was standing right where he had left her.

Snow fell more heavily now, the accumulation startlingly deep already. Bella was wearing flimsy flats. He scooped her into his arms and carried her the short distance to the passenger seat. When she was settled, he closed her door, loped around the car, and slid behind the wheel.

The storm had set in with a vengeance. Visibility was incredibly bad, particularly since he had to concentrate with all his might to stay on the correct side of the road. It wasn't easy with Bella at his elbow.

She gave him directions calmly, apparently unfazed that they had walked out on a fancy-ass dinner and were close to being stranded in a blizzard.

"How much farther?" he asked hoarsely.

"Two more blocks to the next light. Then right on Barker Street. Last house at the end of the cul-de-sac. We don't have my car, so I'll run inside and open the garage."

He didn't like that idea. What if she decided to lock him out? But he didn't have a better suggestion.

The directions were spot on. When he pulled up in her driveway, Bella hopped out before he could protest. Immediately, she was swallowed up in the veils of snow.

The moments between the time she got out of the car and the instant the garage door started to go up were some of the longest of Ian's life. He pulled forward carefully. When he shut off the engine, Bella was waiting for him, standing on the top step that led into the house.

His overcoat was covered in rapidly melting snowflakes.

"Take it off," Bella said, watching him brush the moisture from his sleeves. "I have a coat rack here by the door."

He followed her inside, looking around with interest. Her house was small and old, but everything from the gleaming hardwood floors to the kitchen appliances to the double-paned windows had been immaculately updated. "When did you buy this place?" he asked. "It's charming."

"It's a rental. I've been here for almost two years now while I worked on my degree."

"I see."

Somewhere on the way from the restaurant to Bella's house, they had lost something. He'd been feeling hopeful, but now everything was awkward and stilted again. "What about that pizza you promised?" he said, forcing a smile he didn't feel.

She nodded, her attention on the stack of mail on the counter. "Of course. I'll preheat the oven. Would you like a glass of wine while we wait?"

Bloody hell. This wasn't at all how he wanted things to go. He rounded the small island with the copper sink and put his hand beneath her elbow, needing to touch her. "Can we go into the living room and talk for a few minutes? I have something I want to show you."

"Whatever you like." Bella was wearing her hostess persona. He hated it.

She led him to a small comfy room with a couch and a loveseat and a television mounted on the wall over an old-fashioned fireplace that had been converted to glass logs. With a flip of a switch, cheery red and gold flames danced and sparked.

A small Christmas tree sat in front of the window. Bella bent to plug in the lights and then chose to sit in the armchair near the fire.

Ian sat down as well, frowning and patting the sofa cushion beside him. "Come over here. Please."

She was visibly wary, but she did as he asked. What did she think he was going to do? Pounce on her?

"The snow is getting deeper, Ian," she said. "You should say what you came to say before it gets too bad for you to make it back to your hotel. I assume you're out by the airport?"

"Yes." Damn. Why was this so hard? He pulled his phone from his pocket and clicked on the photo icon. "This is my flat in London. It's very nice actually. I have a view of the Thames."

Bella leaned closer as he flipped quickly. "It's lovely, Ian." She scooted back to her end of the sofa.

"There's more," he said, grinding his jaw.

"Oh. Sorry." She returned to her original spot.

He wanted to use the exact, perfect words. In the end, he simply told her the story. "Two months ago, I approached the couple whose flat occupies the other half of my floor. I offered them 50 percent more than the property was worth, and they accepted. Since then I've knocked out walls and remodeled the entire space. You can see the progress in these next several pictures."

"Okay."

The delicate scent of her perfume made him dizzy. This was the important part. He couldn't afford to choke on the home stretch. "Do you understand what I'm saying, Bella?"

Blue eyes, darker than normal, stared up at him. Her gaze darted from the phone to his face and back again. "I don't believe I do."

Laying the phone aside, he took her hands in his. "I want you to have your own space, the perfect ambience for you to write your novel. I realize that you've completed your dissertation in the time we've been apart, and maybe you've even decided you really wanted to teach. That's not a problem. I'm willing to do whatever it takes." He kissed her nose. "Why do you look so confused? Do you not like the idea? You can be honest with me."

Bella jumped to her feet and paced, her expression harried. "What idea, Ian? What are you saying?"

Well, hell. He'd made a mess of it after all. He took a small velvet box out of his pocket and went down on one knee at her feet. Flipping open the lid, he took a deep breath. "Arabella Margaret Craig. Will you marry me?"

Tears leaked down her cheeks. She didn't even reach for the ring. Instead, she put her hands to her face. "Ian. You can't be serious."

His heart sank. "You fell in love with me once. Won't you give me another chance? I won't ever leave you again."

She sat down on the rug as if her legs had turned to spaghetti. Leaning her head against his chest, she cried.

He put the ring box aside and wrapped his arms around her. "I adore you, Bella. You came into my life and turned everything I thought I knew upside down. These months apart have been a hellish, lonely desert. But I wanted to wait until I could prove that I had room in my life for you, for us. The truth is, though, without you I won't have any kind of life at all."

* * *

Bella didn't want to cry anymore. The weeks of grief and heartache and questions caught up with her, though, and she couldn't stop. The front of Ian's shirt was wet through with her tears.

He held her tightly without speaking, resting his chin on top of her head and murmuring words of Gaelic that sounded much like the ones he had used the last time they made love.

Finally, her sobs dwindled to the occasional hiccup. "I'm sorry," she sniffled. "I'm not usually so emotional."

Ian stroked her hair. "Cry all you want, lass. Your tears are knives in my heart, but I deserve them."

She pulled back far enough to look at his ridiculously handsome face. "I love you, Ian. And for the record, I love you exactly the way you are. Redoing your flat is one thing, but you don't need to change any of the quirks that make *you* you. I would never ask that. I fell for the man with the incredible brain and the terrible fashion sense and the delightful accent that makes it very hard to carry on a serious argument with you."

He wiped a stray tear from her cheek. "That could work in my favor, don't you think?"

She nodded, struggling to accept that this moment was really happening. "Perhaps I could look at that jewelry box again."

He grinned and reached for it. "I wanted something to match your eyes. Though a mere sapphire could never come close."

Bella held her breath as he slid the gorgeous ring onto her finger. It was almost a twin to the one Diana Spencer had made famous and Kate Middleton now wore. The center stone was a deep, brilliant blue, three carats at least, surrounded by a dozen or more perfect diamonds. She held her hand up to the light, loving the way the stones flashed and sparked. "It's beautiful, Ian...stunning actually. I don't know what to say."

"I thought if it was good enough for a princess, it might come close to being good enough for you. I adore you, Bella."

The catch in his voice squeezed her heart. At last, after miserable, lonely weeks of living without him, he was here. He kissed her...gently at first. The taste of him went to her head faster than any wine. "I won't break, Ian." After that, talking went by the wayside. He undressed her while they clung to each other, panting, kissing wildly.

When they were both naked, Ian ran his hands over the gooseflesh on her hip. "We could move to your bed," he said.

She could tell from the tone of his voice he didn't really want to. Neither did she. Inside the house, the fire was crackling...outside, the snow was falling...and here in this small room, all was right with the world.

He took care of protection and then lifted her in his arms, laying her on the sofa and coming down on top of her. "You're mine now," he muttered.

Bella wrapped her legs around his waist and brushed a lock of hair from his damp forehead. "And you're mine," she said. "My dear, impossible genius." When he entered her with one slow, steady thrust, she groaned. "Don't stop," she begged. "Don't ever stop."

He buried his face in her shoulder, his big body shuddering. "I'll not stop until we're both too old and senile to care."

"Then never," she whispered softly, feeling the end rushing at her like a storm that couldn't be escaped. "Never, Ian."

They came at almost the same instant, caught up in aching need from weeks spent apart.

When they could breathe again, Ian lifted up on one elbow, his usually sharp-eyed gaze hazy. "I forgot to ask. May I spend the night?"

"I was counting on it," she said, smugly happy. "I was counting on it."

Chapter Twenty-One

Six months later…

Bella stood in ivory ballet slippers and a fairytale wedding dress just outside the arched doorway that led into St. Margaret's Chapel. The panoramic views of Edinburgh this afternoon were incredible, but she barely spared a glance for the scenery. Fidgeting with the bodice of her gown, she glanced at McKenzie who was stunning in aquamarine silk.

"I feel like I'm going to be sick," Bella muttered.

McKenzie smiled sympathetically. "Wedding nerves. I was the same way. The men have taken their places inside, so it's almost time to go. You look amazing, sweetheart. I *would* hug you, but I don't want to mess up your veil. I spent too long getting it exactly right."

Bella gazed at her sister-in-law with trembling lips, choked by a wave of emotion. "Thank you for being here today. It means the world to me."

The guest list for the chapel was limited to twenty-five. Ian and Bella had realized early on that it would be virtually impossible to start inviting friends without offending someone. For that reason, they had chosen to have a private ceremony instead, with two receptions later, one in London and one in North Carolina.

Today in the chapel, the only participants would be the priest, the two couples, one harpist who would act as witness, and the benign spirt of the departed Saint Margaret. Ian had invited his father, but the older man declined, citing his health. He and Bella had met several times by now and were on good terms.

McKenzie glanced at her watch, opened the door, and smiled reassuringly. "It's time, Bella."

Spilling out into the warm spring sunshine, the lilting notes of the harp filled the alcove with a melodious air from Handel's "Water Music". McKenzie walked slowly toward the front and took her place opposite Finley. Bella lifted her chin, took a deep breath, and followed. Though she knew the confines of the small lovely chapel very well by now, she had eyes only for Ian. He was resplendent today in a dress kilt fashioned from the Larrimore tartan. The crisp white shirt showed off his tan and his broad shoulders.

Afterward, she couldn't remember the steps that took her from the door to the altar of the chapel, but she found herself in exactly the right spot. She handed her bouquet of white roses to McKenzie. Then Ian took both of her hands in his, smiling. She had never seen him look so happy or so much at peace.

The elderly priest nodded his head and began to speak. "Friends, we are gathered here today in the sight of God and these witnesses to join this man and this woman in holy matrimony. In the millennium that has passed since this kirk was built to honor Saint Margaret and to glorify the Almighty, your children have taken shelter in these walls. They have faced the grief of loss. They have weathered the fear of the unknown. Last but certainly not least, they have experienced the boundless joy we celebrate today. I would ask that you bless Ian and Arabella Margaret on this day they are wed. Let us pray…"

Bella experienced some kind of out-of-body experience in those next moments. It was a combination of things perhaps—the scent of lilies on the altar, the feel of Ian's large warm hands enfolding hers, the misty-eyed emotion on her brother's face. The priest's voice rose and fell, repeating ago-old words of faith and commitment.

Ian slid a simple platinum band on her left hand and repeated his vows. She reciprocated in a clear voice, determined not to cry when she was so very, very lucky to be standing in this historic spot with the man of her dreams.

At last, it was over. She had wanted to memorize every moment, but her heart was too full. The priest joined their four hands and placed his on top. The blessing and benediction he offered was in Gaelic, one Ian had suggested. Bella had learned the words by heart, and their meaning. She let the old man's heavy Scottish accent wash over her and fill her with buoyant joy.

Then the pronouncement, a burst of celebratory music from the harpist, and a flurry of hugs and laughter.

While Ian thanked the priest and McKenzie spoke to the harpist, Bella pulled her brother aside. "I wanted to tell you something before Ian and I leave on our honeymoon."

Finley kissed her cheek. "This was a perfect wedding, Bella. You're a gorgeous bride. So tell me. What is it?"

Her cheeks felt hot. "Just a head's up that you may be an uncle sooner rather than later."

He gaped at her. "You're pregnant?"

"Oh, no. Not yet. But Ian's childhood was pretty dreadful. Yours and mine wasn't too much better. We've decided we want a big family, and we don't want to waste any time. Plus, I'll have almost a year to work on my novel even if I get pregnant right away, so that will keep me plenty busy in London."

Finley beamed. "Well, McKenzie didn't want to steal your thunder, but she and I *are* pregnant."

When Bella gasped, he shushed her. "Swear to me you won't let on that I told you. She'd have my hide."

"I won't say a word." Bella hugged him tightly. "Mama would be proud of us, I think."

Finley nodded. "Yep. All things considered, we turned out pretty well."

They turned in unison and gazed at their spouses who were laughing and joking and apparently having a lot of fun together.

Finley lifted an eyebrow. "Should we break up their party?" he joked.

Bella caught her brand new husband's eye and smiled at him. Ian stopped mid-sentence and came to claim his bride. McKenzie followed right behind him, snagged her husband's wrist, and dragged him close for an enthusiastic hug.

Over Ian's shoulder, Bella blew her brother a kiss. "Nothing to worry about, Finley. I have it on good authority that we all lived happily ever after."

If you enjoyed *Scot on the Run* be sure not to miss Janice Maynard's

NOT QUITE A SCOT

McKenzie Taylor is high maintenance when it comes to fashion, but when it comes to travel, the socialite prefers privacy to parties, and her own space to hotels. After she and her friends arrive in Scotland and split up to pursue their own adventures, she rents a small cottage on the Isle of Skye. On day two, she crashes her rental car. But a hero emerges from the mist to rescue her. He's handsome, earthy, funny, and before long is making her feel desirable, not to mention desirous. There's just one problem: McKenzie's Highland dreamboat is a motorcycle riding *American.*

Finley Craig knows his cute new tourist friend is stubbornly set on falling for a Scotsman. But he's just as set on her falling for him. So he plans to give her a taste of what she *thinks* she wants. Because Finley suspects McKenzie isn't as shallow as she appears. And in the process of surrounding her with his hand-picked suitors, she may just decide that American-made is best—especially when she and Finley are rained in together over one long, delicious, and very adventurous weekend…

A Lyrical Shine e-book on sale now!

Read on for a special excerpt.

Chapter 1

Headed for Inverness on the East Coast Train...

Scotland. The Highlands. Purple heather. Northern lights. Men in kilts. I was too excited to sleep. I might have made this journey on my own long ago. Instead, I had waited until the moment was right. The wrong companions could ruin even the most exotic trip. Luckily, I'd known the two women traveling with me since we were all in diapers.

Hayley—whose mother ran the in-home daycare where my friends and I first met as toddlers—taught third grade. She was organized, earnest, and one of the most caring people I'd ever known. It pleased me to see her so happy. She practically vibrated with enthusiasm.

After the long flight from Atlanta to Heathrow—and a brief night of sleep in a nondescript hotel room—the three of us were now sitting in motor coach–style seats on either side of a small rectangular table. The train racketed along at high speeds, stopping now and again to drop off and pick up passengers as we whizzed through the countryside. Hayley had finished her tea and was poring over one of the guidebooks she'd brought along.

Willow, on the other hand, brooded loudly, if such a thing were possible. I suspected her cranky attitude was a cover for very real nerves. She had never traveled farther than a few hundred miles from the Peach State. This was a big step for her, not only because of transportation firsts, but because she'd had to leave her business behind.

The salon she co-owned, *Hair Essentials,* was the product of blood, sweat, and tears. Willow's history was neither as privileged as mine nor as stable as Hayley's. Yet somehow, our cynical friend had managed to find her own path, and a successful one at that.

I stifled an unexpected yawn, swamped by a wave of fatigue. Despite the collection of stamps in my passport, I'd never mastered the art of crossing time zones unscathed.

Willow and I had been squabbling half-heartedly for the last hour. As if sensing that I was losing my steam, she half turned in her seat and glared at me. "Jamie Fraser is a fictional character," she said. "Like Harry Potter or Jason Bourne. You're not going to find him wandering around the Scottish Highlands waiting to sweep you off your feet."

I glared right back at her. "I *know* that. I'm not delusional. But at least I have a whimsical soul. You wouldn't know a romantic moment if it smacked you in the face."

We were in the midst of an ongoing argument that neither of us was going to win. I knew the Harry Potter reference was a deliberate jab at me. Though my travel companions had moaned, I'd awakened them early enough this morning to make it to King's Cross Station for photographs and retail therapy. After all, it wasn't every day I had a chance to get my picture taken at the famous Platform 9 ¾.

By the time I scoured the handkerchief-sized gift shop and braved the line of tourists posing for the platform picture, we'd had mere minutes to make our noon departure. It was worth the mad scramble. I considered J. K. Rowling one of the wonders of the modern world.

Willow wasn't really miffed about my Harry Potter obsession. She was scared…scared that we three were embarking on an outlandish adventure sure to disappoint us in the end. I could see it in her wary gaze. Life—and probably men as well—had not been kind to her.

Hayley looked at Willow and me with hurt, puppy dog eyes, as if stunned we could be at odds in the midst of this great adventure. "You're both jet-lagged," she said. "If you're not going to enjoy the trip, at least get some sleep so you won't be grumpy when we get to Inverness. I'm tired of listening to both of you."

Willow and I tabled our squabbles in favor of closing our eyes. Now the sensation of motion intensified. The train raced along, offering tantalizing glimpses of the countryside each time I peeked. Though I had spent a week in Edinburgh several years ago, this was my first chance to venture north. I had told Willow and Hayley that a recent bequest from my grandmother's estate prompted our bucket list trip, but in truth, I'd been planning this pilgrimage for some time.

I was trying to make up for the decade and a half when my childhood friends and I lost touch. Though Hayley's mom had eventually caught up with most of her daycare graduates via Facebook, in the years before that, little more than Christmas cards kept the connection alive between my friends and me.

Our lives had taken far different paths. Hayley was firmly middle-class America with two loving parents and a conventional job. Willow, on the other hand, didn't talk much about her past. Her father had walked out right about the time my parents pulled me from public school and enrolled me in an elite academy. Willow and her mom had been forced to rely on the kindness of relatives who lived on the opposite side of the city.

Despite our differences and the years we spent apart, we were closer now than ever, partly because of a shared obsession, albeit a harmless one. We were all three madly enamored with Diana Gabaldon's *Outlander* books, and more recently, the TV series. We spent hours critiquing the first season of the show, deciding that although nothing could compare to the actual book, the producers and directors and cast had done a bang-up job of bringing Claire Randall and Jamie Fraser to life.

Somewhere, somehow, in the midst of a sleepless spring night when my hormones were raging and my good sense waning, I had seized on the idea that Hayley and Willow and I should travel to Scotland and seek out our own *Outlander*-style adventures, preferably with a kilt-clad hero involved.

I knew my plan was farfetched. Guys like the fictional Jamie Fraser, particularly in the twenty-first century, were few and far between. I'd dated my share of losers. Kissing frogs was a rite of passage for millennials.

In my personal experience, though, American men tended to fall into three categories: mama's boys who wanted another woman to take care of them; high-powered workaholics who didn't need or care about real relationships; and last but not least, a large group of genuinely nice guys who would make great boyfriend or husband material, but didn't get my heart (or anywhere else) all fizzy.

Still, I couldn't give up hope that somewhere out there was the one man who was my soul mate. I didn't actually share that belief with my friends for several reasons. Hayley lived like a nun, and Willow was too much of a hard-ass to believe in fairytale romance. Or if she *did* believe in it, she sure as heck wouldn't admit to something so *girly*.

My goal for this trip was to get away from everything that pigeonholed me back in the States. I lived mostly in Atlanta, but my parents had a penthouse apartment in New York and a ski chalet in St. Moritz. I was the epitome of the poor little rich girl. I knew my last nanny better than I knew my own mother.

I wasn't complaining. Not at all. Nobody ever said life was fair. Since I'd never had to clip coupons or worry about my car being repossessed, I suppose it made cosmic sense that the average American family wasn't something I would ever have. No Monopoly games around the kitchen table. No making s'mores over a summer campfire. No irritating siblings to steal the attention from me.

Hayley and Willow were the closest thing to sisters I would ever have. I felt more than a little guilty that I had bludgeoned them into making this trip. Even though I paid for the first class airfare and train tickets, the two of them were still going to be out of pocket for lodging and meals.

I wished they would let me cover that, too, but Hayley had pulled me aside months ago and pointed out that she and Willow needed to feel invested in this adventure and not entirely beholden to me. Like Claire Randall, the gutsy heroine of *Outlander*, we were supposed be bold and independent. In the process, perhaps we might stumble upon our own gorgeous, chivalrous, modern-day Highlanders.

Hayley believed it could happen. Willow would probably work hard to make sure it *didn't* happen. And as for me…well, I as far as I was concerned, it was a pleasant daydream.

My repeated yawns were rubbing off on Willow. She pinched the bridge of her nose. "Tell me again why we didn't fly straight to Inverness?"

"You know why," Hayley said. She opened her notebook. "We agreed that since we can't actually go back in time like Claire does in *Outlander*, this train journey will be symbolic of our desire to go off the grid for a month. No cell phones. No Internet. No Facebook. No Twitter. You agreed, Willow."

"Under duress," she muttered.

I snickered. "You're bitchy when you're tired."

"And you're even more annoying than usual," Willow drawled.

Usually, I loved a good argument. At the moment, though, I was not at my best. After a warning glance from Hayley, I pretended to sleep again. Maybe that would keep me out of trouble.

This train ride had turned me inside out. I was flooded with all sorts of feelings. The fact that my two best friends had followed along with my mad scheme humbled me. I would be absolutely devastated if either of them ended up getting hurt, either physically or emotionally.

It wasn't too late to back out. One word from me and I felt sure either or both of my friends would agree to a new course of action, one where we stuck together as a team. Why had *safe* seemed like such a dirty word?

Our plan was to remain together tonight at the hotel adjacent to the train station in Inverness. Then tomorrow morning, we would all three go our separate ways. My stomach clenched and my chest tightened. Whatever happened after that would be all my fault.

Hayley tapped the notebook where she had underlined the final piece of our plan. "And remember—every night at nine o'clock, or as close as we can make it, we'll turn on our phones and check for any emergency messages from each other."

Willow nodded. "I won't forget." I sensed that she was as worried about Hayley as I was. Willow had street smarts, but our schoolteacher friend exhibited a naïve streak a mile wide.

The odd thing was, Willow and I were probably the two with the most in common. Which sounded ridiculous given the circumstances of our upbringing. But it was true.

Hayley possessed the wide-eyed wonder of a child and a nonchalant certainty that people were basically nice and sweet and accommodating. Lord help us if she ever found out that wasn't true.

Then there was Willow: hard-working, gruff Willow. Rough around the edges. Abnormally cautious when it came to money. Almost always expecting the worst. I'm sure she would hoot at the comparison, but she and I shared a similar outlook. Neither of us wanted to depend on anyone else for our happiness and our security.

Willow had coped with poverty and a dysfunctional family. The hand I'd been dealt included too much money and parents who barely acknowledged my existence. I'd long since given up trying to win their approval.

Even if I could go out tomorrow, marry a Wall Street banker, and pop out two point five kids, it still wouldn't be enough. My father's career engulfed him. My mother's vanity and narcissism absorbed her.

Thank God I had two such amazing human beings for friends. I loved both with a raw intensity that would probably astonish each of them in different ways. With seven years of adult friendship under our belts to bolster our childhood memories, I would never let them go. Not the recollections of the past, and certainly not the women themselves.

Hayley and Willow and I were the same age. At the moment, though, I felt the sole burden of responsibility. This entire *Outlander* scheme was *my* idea. If it failed, I'd be to blame. If it succeeded, even on a superficial level, we'd have a thrilling month ahead.

Despite the panic and the second thoughts, the prospect was exhilarating. Was there a Jamie out there for me? A strong, chivalrous Scotsman who would fight for me and keep me warm at night?

I closed my eyes and tried to conjure up his face.

Inverness couldn't get here soon enough...

Meet the Author

Photo by Jamie Pearson Photography

USA Today bestselling author Janice Maynard knew she loved books and writing by the time she was eight years old. But it took multiple rejections and many years of trying before she sold her first three novels. After teaching kindergarten and second grade for a number of years, Janice took a leap of faith and quit her day job. Since then she has written and sold over thirty-five books and novellas.

During a recent trip to Scotland, Janice enjoyed getting to know the "motherland." Her grandfather's parents emigrated from the home of bagpipes, heather, and kilts. Janice lives in east Tennessee with her husband, Charles. They love hiking, traveling, and spending time with family.

Hearing from readers is one of the best perks of the job!

You can connect with Janice at http://www.twitter.com/JaniceMaynard, www.facebook.com/JaniceMaynardReaderPage, http://www. wattpad.com/user/JaniceMaynard, and http://www.instagram. com/JaniceMaynard.

CPSIA information can be obtained
at www.ICGtesting.com
Printed in the USA
LVHW011602020719
623002LV00001B/169/P